Celebrate!

Celebrate!

LESSONS LEARNED FROM
THE WORLD'S MOST ADMIRED ORGANIZATIONS

SCOTT FRIEDMAN, CSP

Westland Ltd

westland ltd
61 Silverline Building, 2nd floor, Alapakkam Main Road, Maduravoyal, Chennai 600095
No. 38/10 (New No.5), Raghava Nagar, New Timber Yard Layout, Bangalore 560026
23/181, Anand Nagar, Nehru Road, Santacruz East, Mumbai 400055
93, 1st Floor, Sham Lal Road, New Delhi 110002

First published by Advantage Quest Publishers, 2012

Celebrate! is published in the Indian sub-continent by westland ltd, 2013

10 9 8 7 6 5 4 3 2 1

ISBN: 978-93-82618-91-1

Inside book formatting and typesetting by Ram Das Lal

Printed at HT Media Ltd., Noida

Acknowledgements

The first acknowledgement of gratitude goes to Nico Dondergoor and Diederick Stoel for that fateful day, April 21, 2011, on a coach in Kuala Lumpur, Malaysia, on the way to tour Petronas Leadership Centre. At the time, I was working on an employee engagement book exploring what the world's most admired organizations were doing to attract and retain employees. Diedrick was Nico's professor, and between the two of them and a little insight from me, the next two days were spent in creating the Celebration brand.

Diederick flew from Amsterdam to Denver for a week in October and helped shape the book. Nico came on board for nine months to research, write and help finish the book. His insights and tenacity were invaluable in making sure the book reached its maximum potential. Thanks, Nico, for your dedication, enthusiasm, and passion! You've got a bright future ahead of you.

A huge debt of gratitude is owed to my editor, Elyn Shindler Moldow, who ended up doing so much more than editing. She turned a bunch of scattered thoughts into a logical flow of ideas that I trust will prove valuable for your company and your life. Elyn also served as a constant source of inspiration as she cheered and celebrated the milestones along the way. Thanks, Elyn. You've brought a wonderful spirit to this project. I hate to think what this book would've looked like without you.

Thanks to Brandon Toropov for his writing expertise and cheerful nature in dealing with changes in direction.

A special thanks to Miyoung Yim for always telling me the truth, and not just what I may want to hear. I so appreciate the hours you spent helping me rework the contents of the book.

Thanks to my faithful, long-time assistant Nancy McGraw for her 'always cheerful' attitude about everything.

Thanks to Jitske Kramer for her playful spirit and cultural expertise. Your piece on culture is one of my favorites in the book.

Much appreciation to Scott Halford for his fascinating piece on the link between the brain and celebration.

Thanks to Hong Yan, Carmen Yung, Julie Conceicao, Soo Kui Peng, Kare Andersen, Eric Chester, Mark Sanborn, Mary Loverde, Melanie Mills, Jana Stanfield, Debra Fine, Brad Montgomery, Daniel Burrus, Sam Silverstein, Shep Hyken, George Walther, Brian O'Malley, Ron Kaufman, Tim Wade, David Lim, Mike Podolinsky, Nishant Kasibhatla, Andrea Malin, Barry and Arlene Hirschfeld, and my sister Wendy Elderkin Friedman for their expertise, support and encouragement along the way.

Thanks to both sets of parents: Art and Fran Friedman and Litamae and David Sher, for sharing in my excitement, and your cheerful attitude in listening to my tales of celebration.

Thanks to Rick Curzon of Key Media, Mel Kleiman of Humetrics, and Dato R. Palan of SMR, for helping to provide HR leaders around the world to survey and interview.

To Dato Palan, thanks for always being so supportive of all the Global Speaker Federation Associations and for being a great partner on many good things. I greatly appreciate your friendship.

Rick, thanks for letting me launch the book at the HR Summit, 2012 and for many years of friendship and inspiring collaboration.

Thanks to Dr Bob Nelson of *1001 Ways to Reward Employees*, for being so generous with your time, material, and advice! The examples you've so generously allowed us to borrow for the book add a nice dimension.

Much gratitude to Chester Elton, for always being so helpful and generous and making such a big difference in the world.

Thanks to Tom Rath for so openly sharing his well-being statistics and for such generosity in using the material.

Thanks to the over 600 of you who filled out the survey, and another 100+ for the interviews.

It took a village to get this book out, and now I'm hoping that many villages will be positively impacted by its contents.

CONTENTS

Introduction

The Celebration Factor

Are you ready to celebrate? Good! After all, life is meant to be celebrated. Celebration can do wonders for you, just as it can do wonders for your organization! So welcome to *Celebrate!* a practical handbook on how to bring more celebration into both your organization and your life.

Based on extensive global research, scores of interviews, and my many years of speaking around the world, this book offers strategies, quips, anecdotes, and proven examples from leading organizations who have effectively created – or who are in the process of creating – a culture of celebration in their workplaces.

I invite you to think of this book as a guidebook, a toolkit, and a source of inspiration. My hope is that you'll find something (or better yet, many things) within these pages that will transform your thinking, your workplace, and even your life. Enjoy the ride – I know I have!

Celebration: It's All in Your Head – Literally!

My team and I have researched people the world over to catalogue our findings for this book. Not surprisingly, we discovered more than a few similarities among people across cultures. The one comment we heard more than any other from those interviewed was that they do not celebrate enough, and that they'd like to change that. That's right: People *want* to add more celebration to their lives.

Current brain research suggests that this desire may be more deeply rooted than we realize. In the following excerpt from *Celebrain! The Brain's Natural Inclination to Celebrate,* researcher Scott G. Halford explains the behavioral and neurological patterns behind our drive to enjoy life, from a scientific perspective:

> We are exquisitely designed for celebration, and we have our brain's architecture to thank for that. The overarching hierarchy of the brain is to maximize reward and minimize danger. Every nanosecond of every day, our brains are scanning the environment to protect us from danger and move us to reward. It's what we call in the neuroscience world a 'toward' state, because we move toward that [good] feeling.
>
> When people live in a spirit of celebration, they look for reasons to happy dance, even if only silently. It becomes a way of being, and [then] a habit.

The fact that we are naturally drawn *towards* a 'reward' state, or a state ripe for celebration, punctuates the ease with which we can learn to access and enjoy a better state of mind and life if we're open to it. Soon you will learn more ways to set your inner sail towards your own natural state of positive thinking – which in turn will encourage others to do the same. It's a great way to affect change, and everybody wins!

Celebrating the Companies We Keep...

The information in *Celebrate!* has been gathered from some of the world's most admired companies across many industries. We've collected interviews and surveys from more than 600 people in 35 countries. In terms of position breakdown, 24 per cent of our respondents were CEOs, presidents, and founders of companies; 20 per cent were human resource managers; 11 per cent were human resource directors; and the rest included administrators, consultants, assistant managers, and others.

From an age perspective, our participants comprised a multi-generational group, with 51 per cent ranging between 40 and 60 years in age, 25 per cent in their thirties, and 15 per cent in their twenties. The remaining 9 per cent, the over-60 crowd, deserve extra-special thanks for the many years of celebratory experience they've shared with us.

We are deeply grateful to all our contributors for their generosity of time and spirit. Because of them, you now hold a tool that will serve you and your company for years to come.

On Your Mark, Get Set... to Celebrate!

By using the techniques presented in *Celebrate!* you will be well on your way towards greater creativity and productivity, more engaged employees, better team performance, and enhanced well-being for all. You'll also find many tools you can put to use immediately – both within the workplace and far beyond. Plus, you'll get to have some good old-fashioned fun, both in the reading of this book and in the carrying out of its practices.

Be aware that you may have to toss away some of your existing ideas about celebration as you read on. I know I did. In fact, the biggest surprise to me as I reviewed the research was the part celebration can play in coping with failure or mistakes. A number of times, our test group emphasized how failures can and should be *celebrated!* In doing so, we are able to highlight lessons learned, which in turn can serve as a powerful catalyst towards making new and more productive choices.

In my (most humble) opinion, no current book on this topic offers a more unique or universally relevant angle to employee engagement than does *Celebrate!* And in my less humble opinion, none is more fun to read or to put into practice!

Through this book, you will come to understand the deeply nourishing and fully transformative properties of 'Vitamin C'−Celebration! Soon enough you will see for yourself that a healthy dose of this 'vitamin', when administered mindfully and heartfully, will raise your organization – along with yourself – to unprecedented levels of well-being, productivity, and success... one celebration at a time.

Yours in Celebration,

Scott Friedman, CSP

Chapter 1 Celebration Defined

MORE THAN A WORD

So what do I mean by 'celebration'?

For most people, a celebration is a party. Nothing wrong with a good party, I always say... but there's so much more. One of Webster's many definitions of the word **celebration** is 'a festivity meant to honor or mark a person or an event.' Okay, so now we're getting closer. Another definition is 'an act or example of rejoicing.' That's good, too!

But for the purposes of this book, as well as for the results I hope it will inspire, I'd like to invite you to consider a new definition. To me, it's as simple as this: **Celebration is a state of mind.**

Or, to put it another way: **Celebration is acknowledging that which is good.**

And you might be surprised to realize how much in life is good – if that's where you place your focus.

Whale of a Good Time

It was a beautiful August day in Ketchikan, Alaska. I was hired to be the closing speaker for the Alaska Hospital and Healthcare Association on a cruise ship from Ketchikan to Juneau, where many of the attendees would catch their flights home. It had been a good convention in Ketchikan, and I was honored to be concluding the convention aboard what I'd imagined would be a luxury liner to Juneau.

The harbor was beautiful; however, instead of the nice, relaxing, luxurious cruise ship I'd envisioned, a big, old, drab-looking ferry creaked at the dock, and attendees from the conference were boarding it. Wait – would I really be speaking on that tub? Guess so! All right, then. No problem. *I'm a professional, and all I need is a good mic and a place to stand. Right?* I talked myself out of any concerns I may have had.

So I boarded with our group, which was sharing the boat with many other tourists from around the world. *Bon Voyage* was only ten minutes away; in another twenty, it would be time for the closing speaker (me). Again, no problem! I'd have plenty of time to set up the stage and test the mic. Right?

What a beautiful 'blue sky' kind of day to motivate caregivers in Alaska! We left the dock, and now – with the clock swiftly ticking down to my speech – it was time to find the room, set up the stage, and test the mic.

Suddenly, over a buzzing loudspeaker, a rough voice announced, 'If you want to listen to the speaker, please come to the inside deck. If not, please move to the outside deck. If you do sit inside, please keep your conversation to a minimum.'

What?

Keep your conversation to a minimum?

Inside deck? Outside deck?

But what about my private room?

I was led to the front of the (very public) deck and was handed a 'push-to-talk' two-way communication system. Worse, it was the same PA system our rough-voiced friend had used! And, as if that weren't bad enough, I was then warned that I'd need to stop talking during the announcements. Not to worry, though – no one announcement would last longer than thirty seconds. Yikes! *Note to self: Don't ever accept a speaking date on a big old drab-looking ferry with a loud, buzzing PA system.*

So, there I was, out on an open deck on the beautiful Bering Sea, clumsily holding a push-to-talk mic that could be interrupted at any moment, talking to an audience focused mostly on the scenery, and painfully realizing that half of this audience had absolutely NO clue who I was or, for that matter, what all the hoopla was around this so-called Alaska Hospital and Healthcare Association. How could this possibly turn out well?

What the heck – I'm a seasoned pro. I can handle this! I pushed the button to start the show. Press, talk, release; press, talk, release; press, talk, release ... breathe in, breathe out ... press, talk, release ... time my breaths with each release ... now, if I could just remember, what was I here to talk about?

Had the entire talk lasted three minutes, I would have been fine. Let's just say my thumbs should have had a personal trainer to prepare for this button-pushing marathon. *Stay strong,* I told myself. I still had fifty-five minutes to go in my sixty-minute speech. And then, all of a sudden, a loud commotion rose up to my left, near the window. People yelled and pointed, and then what seemed like the entire audience stood up, rushed to the window, and stood in awe at ... a pod of whales jumping out of the water! They were playing feverishly, totally unaware of the speaker on the main deck trying to hold the attention of the audience. (Tell me, how do you compete with eleven whales a jumpin'? You don't.) So, if you can't beat 'em, join 'em, right? Count the whales, win a prize, collect the whole set!

My dear audience was having a whale of a good time celebrating the spontaneity of one of Mother Nature's finest moments. Who was I not to join in the fun? So I created a contest to see who could first spot the whales. Not only did the conference members love it, but the rest of the travelers also became just as eager to get in on the fun. In truth, those whales saved me from the difficulty of the moment. Because I saw them as an opportunity rather than a nuisance, I was able to capture the moment for the benefit of everyone. And that just it: it's all about creating that celebration mindset.

YOUR CELEBRATION MINDSET

Sure, maybe it's easier to find joy in jumping whales rather than in a sore thumb, but either way, you've got to consciously choose that celebration mindset.

So what does this mindset entail? It's about finding the good in the present moment; it's focusing on what you want more of in your life; it's enjoying the journey, even when the journey doesn't seem worthy of enjoying. It's choosing to appreciate the moments – right along with those who share the moments with you.

That's exactly what happened to me on that trip to Juneau! And now I have a NEW note to self: *If you see a rickety (but well-built) boat creaking by the dock, make haste to board it! You never know...*

Celebration is (Joyful) Work

Keep in mind, though, shifting your thinking towards the positive will only work if *you* do. And the first order of business is to open yourself to the ways of that **celebration mindset** I've mentioned – the one that's all about bringing more richness into our lives by creating more moments of joy. It's celebrating lessons learned and people in our lives. It's creating rituals that honor who we are, as well as who others are. It's our dreams and others' dreams. It's celebrating achievements, advancements, and as many of life's moments as we possibly can.

It's about having more joy and less hassle in our lives. Nice concept, eh? Here's how I learned about it:

The 'Hassle and Joy' Factor

I was on an evening flight from Denver to Nashville. I decided to strike up a conversation with my seatmate.

'I'm Scott.'

'Hi, I'm John.'

'Do you live in Nashville?'

'Just outside of town on a ranch. And you?'

'Denver.'

'What do you do, John?'

'I'm a musician.'

'A famous musician?' I asked jokingly.

'Not sure about famous, but we did get lucky, and we wrote two songs that launched our careers in a big way.'

'Really,' I said, interested. 'What were the songs?'

'Born to Be Wild' and *'Magic Carpet Ride.'*

'Born to be WILLLLLD', I sang badly, but I couldn't remember who had actually recorded it. Where is that airline internet connection to access Google when you need it?

John saved me the embarrassment of having to ask by reintroducing himself.

'Hi, I'm John Kay, of John Kay's Steppenwolf.'

I was sitting next to a rock legend!

For the next hour or so, we talked about life – about such things as joy and what's really important. At one point, John told me, 'We price our band's services based on the "hassle and joy" factor. We look at how much hassle it would be for us to do the gig and how much joy it would bring us. In the summertime, my kids are out of school, and there are many fun things to do on the ranch. I really don't like leaving the family and the ranch; it's a hassle. So the price of the band goes up. But if it's a place that brings me great joy, the price of booking the band goes down. Then, in the wintertime when the kids are back in school, it's not such a hassle to leave Nashville, and the price of the band goes down. I make decisions in my life based on the "hassle and joy" factor.'

Wow! Not only was I sitting next to a rock legend, I was sitting next to a rock legend who had found a simple, practical guide to living life. I could already see my new favorite t-shirt: *He or she who dies with the most joys, wins!*

Okay, so it sounds easy enough. But in a tough economy, with lots of stress and a family to raise, is it *really* that easy? My (simple) answer is *Yes.* I know at times life may be difficult, yet ultimately, we get what we focus on.

What the World Needs Now... is Celebration

The reality is, this shift in thinking is needed now more than ever. As individuals in a global community, we seem to have more stress than ever before. Unemployment rates are high, and morale is low. We're all feeling the pressure of pressure. Life is hard ... that is, if we let it be. The good news is this: We don't have to let it be.

When I was twenty years old, I lost a brother who was twenty-one. Not only was Brett my brother, he was also one of my closest friends. It was the first time someone close had been taken from me. The unparalleled loss led me to question so many things in life. Most of all, it forced me to review my priorities in a completely different light. I asked myself: *What's really important?*

Almost overnight, I was forced to grow up. Life as I knew it before the tragedy had vanished. If there was a silver lining, it was this: Never again would I take life for granted. I realized how fragile life is, how important and fleeting each moment is. In time, I also came to realize that the worst things in life contain the seeds of the best, if only we're open to learning and growing from them.

A Shift in Thinking = A Shift in Being

Celebration is about acknowledging all that is good in your life. Even what may appear to be tragedy in your life can be shifted into good if we focus on the gifts to be discovered and the lessons to be learned.

If you're reading this book, you must be curious about celebration and the potential impact it may have in your life. On the other hand, you might be reading it to prove me wrong and to justify your state of misery. May I assume it's the first reason? Good! It'll make for better reading, I promise.

To gain the most from this book, I ask you to read it with a commitment towards honoring your life through celebration. That's right – when you find yourself on a ferry with a sore thumb, you must be willing to look for the whales. I realize that this is not an easy intentional shift to make, but doing so will pay off well beyond the moment. It will affect your life profoundly in the days and years to come.

Your First Celebration Assignment

So are you ready for your first exercise of the book? Here it comes: The 'Celebration Scale.' Give it a try!

On a scale of 1-10, with 1 corresponding to a complete lack of celebration in your life, and 10 indicating that your life is full of celebration, where would you say you are right now? Where would you like to be?

Let this be your 'Celebration Project' – one you can take with you when you leave this book. Consider it your commitment to going from where you are now on the Celebration Scale to where you want to be. This book will give you ideas on how to make the shift, both in the workplace and beyond.

Life is a Series of Choices

You are where you are today based on the choices you've made up to this point, and you will be where you are tomorrow based on the choices that you make today. If you want to change the future, change your choices. **One of the most important choices you can make is to celebrate life more!** Why not focus less on being successful, and more on successfully being?

This book is about *allowing* life to be easier. How? By learning to make celebration a way of living, thinking, contributing, and *being,* rather than just a mantra we remind ourselves to act upon from time to time.

The road to happiness becomes much easier and brighter when you choose a celebration mindset. For truly, the road to happiness is paved with celebration.

So What Do You Say?

Are you ready to look for the whales? Are you ready to create more joy and less hassle in your life? Are you ready to build a workplace, a career, and a life of celebration? If so ... turn the page.

Chapter 2

A Journey into the Celebration Mindset

My mother's biggest stress for as long as I can remember has been trying to get me married off. Not long ago, she said, 'Scott, because you travel so much, maybe the future Mrs Friedman lives in another city. You know what you should do? You should try one of those internet dating services! You know the kind – Match.com, Loveforlife.com, willyoupleasemarrymyson.com.'

Well, I happened to have an extra night in Boston on an upcoming speaking engagement, so I thought, why not please my mother? Who knows, something good may happen. I figured, all you have to do is log onto the site, fill out a questionnaire, enter what you're looking for in a mate, provide credit card information, and – *poof!* – just like magic, you have potential dates. It's a beautiful concept, is it not? Sure it is! So I did just that, and then the fear struck – fear that the system would read my entry and say, 'No service provided; NO DATE FOR YOU!!'

Luckily, that didn't happen. On the contrary, over 200 possible dates came back for Boston. I only had one night. You can play the fantasy in your mind, but you know it isn't going to work.

So I thought, what am I going to do? I'm getting close to the date for my Boston engagement. How many emails will I need to send to get my one date? Then I reasoned: 'I'm a decent guy, I've got a good heart, I'm not the axe-murdering type (thankfully). So if I send out six requests, shouldn't I be able to come up with one date?' No need to answer.

Well, three of my prospects didn't respond at all. The fourth one called me 'geographically undesirable' – Denver/Boston, over 1500 miles – fair enough. The fifth one said I was 'chronologically undesirable,' which means I'm too old ... ouch ... and here I thought I was just boyishly mature! The sixth one just checked the 'No' box. Okay, not a big deal. I've had my 'No' box checked many times over the years.

But now what to do? What do YOU do in a situation where things don't quite match the Master Plan? And how, in a situation like this, do we keep that celebration mindset? Let me help.

ESTABLISHING THE GPS

In one of our survey questions, we asked our respondents, 'What is essential in making a celebration successful?' Time and again, three words were mentioned: **gratitude, play, and surprise**. GPS!

So exactly what do these words mean, and how do we apply them to my Boston dating experience?

Let's start with simple definitions fitting for this context:

Gratitude – An appreciation for all the good things we have in our life.

Play – Having fun, creating humor, and being experimental in the present moment.

Surprise – Including the element of the unexpected.

So I turned on my 'GPS'. I wrote to Becky, the one who said I was chronologically undesirable. I needed to prove to her that the best things in life are sometimes ... just a little bit older.

> *Dear Becky,*
>
> *I'm writing to inform you that I reject your rejection. I appreciate the time it took to reject me, but at this time, I'm taking no turn-downs of any sort. I'll see you Saturday night. Dress casually, and please email me directions to your favorite restaurant or your house.* (Hey, you never know. She just may go with it!)

And so, the happily-ever-after unfolds this way:

> *Dear Scott,*
>
> *It appears you have a sense of humor. And for your guts and your persistence, here are directions to my house.*

Woo hoo! I followed the directions she'd given to her house, and it turned out to be ... her house! Who would've thought? We went out in Boston and had a great time. Since then, she's been to Denver three times, I've been to Boston three times, and – believe it or not – we just took a cruise for her grandmother's 85th birthday! Now I'm happy to announce that this is the lady I will marry.

Okay, maybe it COULD'VE happened that way. And maybe you've heard about such fairy-tale-like endings happening to people like me all the time. The truth is, SHE NEVER WROTE BACK. Why, I wondered? Maybe she found me just deleteful? If only she'd turned on her GPS! Then we might have celebrated a life of wedded bliss together and lived 'happily ever laughter.'

Which leads me to ask, how many opportunities have we missed in our lives because we never bothered to turn on our GPS?

It's no mystery why certain organizations have great success in creating a culture of celebration. They've turned on their GPS – their sense of Gratitude, Play, and Surprise – and what a difference this has made. Before we dig into specifics, let me illustrate a time when a company's GPS was on in full force, not to mention in full color.

Pink Party

We interviewed the General Manager of a five-star hotel with years of managing experience all over the globe. This is someone who fully understands the importance of taking care of your employees. He knows how to engage and connect with people from any culture. His goal is to create a culture wherein his employees feel comfortable talking to him about anything.

He tells the story of the time Britney Spears visited the hotel decked out in pink. ALL pink: pink mini-skirt, pink pumps, pink purse, pink lips – she was pretty much a pink party. The hotel staff took wonderful care of her, just as they do of all their guests. Of course, behind the scenes, the staff good-naturedly kidded about the Pink Party. Lots of 'pinkin'-thinkin' going on.

Shortly after Britney's visit, the GM went on vacation for his birthday.

Upon his return ten days later, he couldn't believe his eyes. Was he suffering from 'pink-eye', or had his office been completely transformed into a party of pink? Pink crepe paper covered the filing cabinets, phone and fax. The desk was draped in pink, with pink pens, pink clips, and a pink nameplate. Even the walls had been painted... yes, pink. It took the GM ten minutes to pop his way to his desk through a parade-path of pink balloons. *Pop, pop, pop* ... ahhh, so there's my desk!

Now, imagine if you had been the GM in this situation? Would you have loved it or hated it? Well, this GM loved it, and here's why: In order for his employees to have the nerve to go to such extremes with their own 'pink party', they had to feel a deep level of trust and connection. They had to know without a doubt that they were truly part of a very caring family. How else could they have found the nerve to pink-ify their boss's private space?

What a perfect example of GPS in action to create a workplace celebration!

Now, let's take a closer look at this GPS system, and explore ways to apply it in your life and work.

GRATITUDE

From the moment you wake up, practice turning on your GPS for immediate direction. You can't take any chances that you may end up in a ditch with that GPS lady screaming, 'Recalculating, recalculating ...'

So here's a question for you. In general, do you appreciate or depreciate the people and things in your life? Do you look for what's good, or do you dig for what's not? When we complain, when we depreciate, when we focus on what *isn't* working in our lives, we let the clouds of negativity block the sunshine of gratitude. Where there's a grudge, anger, or resentment, there's no space for gratitude. As Don Ginn once said, 'Gratitude brings about an awakening of the heart to love.'

Knowing this, how do you create the 'attitude of gratitude' in yourself and your employees?

Let's Get Personal

Every morning when you awake, ask yourself this question: **What am I grateful for today?** If you can't think of anything, check in the obituary section of the newspaper. If your name is not there, there's something to be grateful for. Food on the table, close relationships, health, a job, security, the air you breathe, a sunset, love in your heart – these are just a few gifts we often overlook. Pretend every few weeks that everything is taken away from you, then given back. Appreciate what you've been given and what you've created. Celebrate yourself and your many blessings!

When you count your blessings, you'll find you have many to count, and more will continue to come your way.

Gratitude Journal

Keep a little notebook by your bed. Every night, write down three things for which you are grateful. Don't forget to include those things that didn't work, and be grateful for them, too. They provide a valuable chance to learn life's glorious lessons. We learn so much more from what goes wrong than we do from what goes right.

Practice Gratitude Instead

Next time you feel sad, practice gratitude. Next time you feel fear, practice gratitude. Next time you feel resentment, practice gratitude. Next time you feel anger, practice gratitude. Next time you feel impatient, practice gratitude.

Appreciation is the fastest way to dissolve any negative emotion and to transform your life into something more beautiful. Increase your appreciation, and you will enrich your life... guaranteed!

'Feel Good' File

Keep a colorful container filled with symbolic reminders of all that you're grateful for in your life: certificates of accomplishments, birthday cards, love notes from a spouse or admirer, children's drawings, loving tweets, favorite emails, etc. When you're stressed or pressured, open the container and remember all the wonderful things in your life. Notice how your mood shifts towards gratitude!

Gratitude at Work

Employee Appreciation Days

Approach every day as though it's Employee Appreciation Day. In other words, cultivate that attitude of gratitude for your employees. Show it; *mean* it!

'Cooking up' Some Appreciation

Why not let the leaders cook breakfast, lunch, or even dinner while everyone else relaxes, enjoys, and feels appreciated? After all, the way to an employee's heart is though his or her stomach, right? Food, just about any way you serve it up, is going to create an instant celebration.

'Post-It' Parties

Write down as many nice things as you can about the person or team you're celebrating, and start posting. Post on a computer monitor, a filing cabinet, a map on the wall, a family photo, or anywhere else in the unsuspecting recipients' spaces. Give yourself a time frame, such as two minutes per cubicle. Here are some examples: 'Swee Lin, fast work and clear report on the Perkins account!' – 'Team: great call last night!' – 'Barb, what did you put in those brownies? So delicious! Thanks.'

Customer Gratitude

I spent my last birthday in Kuala Lumpur, Malaysia, at the Sol Melia Hotel – a client and sponsor of one of my personal affiliations, an organization called *Together We Can Change the World* (TWCCTW.org). Arno Thony, the general manager and a good friend of mine, told me they had a treat for me in celebration of the work we're doing together. He would serve dinner for the very first time atop the hotel in a charming little spot which features an unobstructed view of the famous Petronas Twin Towers, as well as of the Kuala Lumpur Water Tower.

Arno told me, 'Choose your favorite meal from this menu, invite up to three friends, and we'll do the rest.' So I asked three good friends, including an American buddy and two others from Malaysia and Korea, to join me for what turned out to be a heavenly meal: tasty tuna sashimi with just the right amount of garlic, Caesar's Salad, steak with a delicious peppercorn glaze, nice-sized lobster tails, and the grand finale – scrumptious chocolate birthday cake. My perfect meal. Yum!

Being pampered for two and a half hours with great wine and great friends made for one of my most memorable birthdays. This illustrates the truth that the deeper the emotion involved in your customers' experiences, the longer they – and you – will remember them. I know that Arno and I will be friends for a long, long time.

Keeping this in mind, how are you thanking your customers – both the ones that you serve inside and those outside the organization?

Thank You, in Writing

A 'Happy Birthday' Facebook post is common. A handwritten thank-you note is not, which is why it gets more attention now than ever. Why not send out two or three thank-you notes per week, or for that matter, per day? How do you feel when you get a handwritten note? Many people keep personal notes in their feel-good files for years!

Kim Mattei of the Believe in Yourself Spa in Denver, Colorado, makes a commitment every year to send out 100 cards of gratitude to people who make a difference in her world – people such as her dentist, doctor, manicurist, children's teacher, school secretary, hair stylist, postal carrier, friend, relative, etc. In other words, if you're in this woman's life, you're probably getting a note of gratitude. Nice, isn't it?

Best of the Best

The following gem of an idea – useful and beneficial both in and out of the workplace – comes from MaryLoverde.com.

Want to create an instant sense of gratitude while connecting with those around you? Play 'The Best of the Best'. Mary created this game as a way to help her kids stay in a place of gratitude over dinnertime conversation. In play, it sounds something like this: What's the best thing that happened at school today? What was the best thing you learned? What was your best laugh?

After a while, your brain begins to naturally scan your experiences looking for those positive elements that keep us grateful. For Mary's kids (as for any of us), this leaves little room for complaining – or for casting those clouds of ingratitude over valuable family time. And guess what? It works just as well in company meetings.

See for yourself. At your next meeting, notice how often people launch into their issues about things that are going wrong. This makes it almost impossible for anyone to focus on gratitude. But you can turn this thinking (and unproductive chatter) right around. Start by asking a question such as, 'What's the best thing that happened since we last met?' or 'Can someone please share a positive customer experience this month?' or maybe 'Who can share a recent experience where an employee went above and beyond for another employee?'

Seeking the best of the best sets a positive, grateful tone for the rest of the meeting. It's a game that's also a game-changer!

Case in point: When I was President of the National Speakers Association in 2004-05, I had the good fortune of traveling to thirty-five state chapters and seven international associations. On many occasions, I would go to dinner with the board of directors the night before a meeting. Sometimes I knew the folks; other times I did not. In either case, I often suggested that we play the Best of the Best. From 'What are you excited about either personally or professionally?' to 'What's your favorite aspect of this business?' to other questions with a positive spin, the game was an ideal way to become acquainted with people in the context of gratitude. And Mr Negative, who many times likes to dominate a dinner conversation, had no choice but to remain quiet. Guess he realized he wasn't invited to this party!

According to Don Ginn, 'Celebration, in the highest sense, is an elegant combination of joy, love, and gratitude. It serves as a vehicle for the very essence of life to flow through us and share its gifts with the world.'

PLAY!

Create some fun. Experiment. Live in the moment. Be curious and spontaneous. Look for the laughs! When you're experimenting in the moment, you have no outside demands, no worries, no pressure… just good, stress-free fun.

Let's take a look at how to strategically use 'play' at work.

Ready to Play

Can you imagine yourself coming to work ready to play? Well, why not start tomorrow, or right now? Smile a lot (people will wonder what you're up to), sing to yourself, sing out loud, hum, skip, dance, learn a magic trick or two, bring props to work, and have some fun. I carry an extendable fork on every trip I take and use it whenever I get the chance. I'll tease a seatmate on an airplane about eating their food or use it at a banquet dinner to add a bit of levity to the main course. Collect little toys and gimmicks and be ready to play whenever the opportunity presents itself (and sometimes even when it doesn't!).

A Funny Thing Happened at Work …

A great way to share the play is to create humor rituals in the workplace. I know – you're busy and don't have a lot of time to waste. But I also know that if you're too busy to play, you're too busy. A quick 'play' break will pay off in greater creativity and productivity. How to set the stage? Some companies will go out on a limb to bring this philosophy to life.

'Get in Touch with your Inner Child' Day

Remember your childhood? Okay, for some of us, it's a long look back. We laughed all the time, and we woke up with a sense of wonder, excited to explore the adventures of the day. Our creativity knew no bounds. What happened to those days?

The management of a government agency in Washington State, according to Jolene Selby (whom we interviewed), was determined to bring back that child-like state in their employees... well, at least once a year.

On this day each year, all employees are encouraged to wear their pajamas to work – appropriate ones, that is. The day starts with Captain Crunch and Cocoa Puffs (feel free to substitute your own favorite kids' foods here). Cartoons run continuously in the break room, where anyone can stop by and tap into his or her inner child. Candy and kids' snacks are available throughout the day. Afternoon breaks include games such as *Pin the Tail on the Donkey* and other old standards. Sing-alongs could include:

- *Head, Shoulders, Knees and Toes*
- *Hokey Pokey*
- *The Bunny Hop*
- *Little Rabbit Foo Foo*
- *My Bonnie Lies Over the Ocean* (while standing up and then sitting down every time you hear a word with the letter 'B' in it)

And at the end of the day, it all ends with a giant pillow fight (be gentle here, please!). Employees are *expected* to be silly and kid-like and to say goodbye to their adult worries of the day (a nice thing to say goodbye to, any day!).

Welcome back your curiosity, sense of adventure, and playful spirit, as you approach the day's opportunities through the eyes of a child.

'Smile! It's Red Friday!' and More Ideas for Theme Days

Having a 'Get in Touch With Your Inner Child Day' is just one (excellent) example of how to create a day for celebration. Hosting a theme day is a wonderful way to usher in the spirit of play for your organization. Looking for more potential themes? Here are several exhilarating candidates:

'Because I Care' Day

Give extra-special treatment to your family and colleagues on this day. There are so many ways you can do this – think kind notes, chocolates, special foods, little gifts, etc. You can post photos, notes and/or pictures in colleagues' offices, catch them doing something right, bake for them, sing to them and, most importantly, just show them you care.

'Remembering Elvis' Birthday Party

Although he is not with us physically, the music of Elvis is still very much alive! On this special day, his songs might be played in the office, your colleagues (and you) may be sporting tight white suits with sequins and rhinestones, and you may be eating banana pudding (Elvis's favorite dessert!). This may be the only day of the year that you have permission to shake your pelvis ... for Elvis.

New Moon, New You

New Moon, new opportunities. From ancient lore to modern-day mysticism, the new moon has been said to mark a new season and a new beginning for you. It's the perfect time to reinvent yourself in any way needed. Today you have permission to imitate Michael Jackson's *Moon Walk*, and no one can criticize you... that is, unless you do that one move.

'Team Spirit' Day

Create some friendly competition by wearing your favorite team's jersey before the big game. It's a great way to connect – both with your mates from your country and with those from other countries. Make some fun bets – such as having the losing team's supporters agree to provide a surprise treat for the winners.

Thank Goodness It's Monday, Friday, or the Second Tuesday of the Month!

As celebrations go, the sky's the limit on this day! Some possible celebrations for a day like this include the Summer Solstice, the Winter Solstice, a 'No Meetings This Week' Day, Election Day, a 'Shave Your Head' Day, etc. (See the list of 'Made-up holidays', below, for more ideas.)

'Employee's Choice' Day

Each employee gets to choose one day a year to call his or her own day. This day could be a birthday or another day that holds a special meaning. Which day would be yours? You're only limited by your imagination on what it is you're celebrating, and what's most appropriate to make it happen.

'Get Fresh with Me' Day: Spring Cleaning!

Cleaning is more fun if you do it together! Put on some energizing music, and dance with your favorite vacuum cleaner (just like Freddy Mercury did in the *I Want to Break Free* music video!). Get the gang even more invested by allowing each person to pick one item from the throw/give-away pile to give as a 'white elephant' – style gift to someone else on the cleaning team. After all, one person's trash is another's treasure, right? When the cleaning's all done, the group can then celebrate by drawing numbers and having a fun gift-choosing celebration!

'Dress Up Like a Nerd' Day

Everyone is allowed – even expected – to be a nerd today. (This should be easy for some... including me!) Put on your thickest glasses, an old sweater from your grandfather, your mother's bobby socks, or pants that are WAY too short. Complete the look by not doing – or over-doing (remember Brylcreem ?) – your hair before you come to work. You might even want to show off your hand-stitched mug warmers at lunch or get into a deep discussion about sci-fi action figures.

'Back to the Future' Day

Set your clocks forward, because today it's going to be the year 2415 at the office! How will you dress? Will you sport purple hair, or will you come in your shiny robot attire? Let your imagination go wild. And don't think you can send in your clone that day. By then, your boss is going to know the difference.

'Color My World' Day

Pick a color, any color. On the designated day, everyone must wear that color. Those who don't must pay a fine, which then helps fund your CSR efforts.

The Cleverest Ritual in All the Land

How about having a contest to come up with the 'Cleverest Ritual' Day? From a 'secret' handshake in the hallway to a pre-meeting cheer, there are endless ways to cleverly connect, honor, and play with your team.

'Bring Your Pet to Work' Day

I know, you're thinking, *Is he crazy? All those pets running around on the same day?* Good point. But how about just one pet per week or month? That way, everyone gets to meet each other's beloved furry friends. (This is assuming your pet has fur, rather than scales or feathers – in which case you might want to get clearance before sending Sally the Snake slithering through the cubicles.)

Fun aside, check your local laws, along with your employees' tolerance, before proceeding with such a day. With care and consideration, it can be a nice way to get to know your colleagues a little better. For instance, that quarterback-sized guy in HR might seem a little less intimidating once everyone meets Louise, his miniature French poodle.

'Mission Possible' Day

Celebrate the mission of the organization through evaluation of its symbols, rituals, pictures, objects, music, stories of heroes and heroines. Today is the day we honor where we've been and where we are going. Questions to ask may include these: *Is our mission still relevant to what we do? Is our company logo still in line with our current mission? Is it attractive? Am I attractive? Oh never mind, it doesn't matter ...*

This may be the perfect time to discuss the company culture at length. What elements have shaped our culture? Who are our heroes? Who are the 'villains'? Tread lightly here. Tell the stories, share the symbols, toast the memories!

And the List Goes On...

The possibilities for celebration days are endless. The list below offers a few more ideas to add to your calendar:

- Casual Friday
- Football Friday
- Bagel Tuesday
- Proud to be Wrong(ly Dressed) Day

- Go Green Day – wear green and celebrate being environmentally conscious
- Funny Hat Monday
- Friday Night Happy Hour (at a new spot each week)
- Pink-Tie Thursday
- Traditional Country Costume Wednesday

And yet more for your celebrating pleasure:

Hooray for Holidays!

If you look at holidays from a global perspective, every day is a holiday! Lucky you if you are living in Japan or India. According to research from Mercer (2009) these countries have 16 public holidays per year – the most of any countries. On the other hand, the UK, the Netherlands, and Australia have the least – eight holidays per year.

Here's an idea: Why not honor the cultural diversity of your work force by celebrating every holiday that your employees celebrate? Get creative as to how you do it. One of my favorites comes from Russia. Have you ever heard of pancake week?

Maslenitsa stems from ancient times and is celebrated for one week in February. As you might have guessed, it is a favorite public holiday for many. During this week, people eat pancakes every day. There are also masquerades, snowball fights, sledding, riding on swings, and plenty of sleigh rides. Go ahead and plan your next spring holiday to Russia, or just bring a little Russia to your company with a pancake celebration!

Pick a Holiday, Any Holiday

The list of holidays below can be found on the most unique of calendars all over the world. How about choosing one or two to celebrate with your organization this year?

Made-up holidays

- **Opposite Day – January 25**
  http://holidayinsights.com/moreholidays/January/oppositeday.htm
- **Insane Answering Machine Day – January 30**
  http://www.holidayinsights.com/moreholidays/January/inanemessage.htm
- **Return-Carts-to-the-Supermarket Month – February 1-28**
  http://www.awarenessmonths.com/2012/01/think-ahead-national-return-shopping-carts-to-the-supermarket-month/
- **Wave-All-Your-Fingers-At-Your-Neighbor Day – February 7**
  http://www.holidayinsights.com/moreholidays/February/wavefingers.htm
- **Fly a Kite Day – February 8**
  http://holidayinsights.com/moreholidays/February/kiteflyingday.htm
- **Blame Someone Else Day – February 13**
  http://holidayinsights.com/other/blamesomeoneday.htm

- **Compliment Day – March 1**
  http://www.worldcomplimentday.com/
- **Make-Up-Your-Own-Holiday Day – March 26**
  http://www.holidayinsights.com/moreholidays/March/makeholidayday.htm
- **Name Yourself Day – April 9**
  http://www.holidayinsights.com/moreholidays/April/nameyourselfday.htm
- **Look-Alike Day – April 20**
  http://www.holidayinsights.com/moreholidays/April/lookalikeday.htm
- **International Dance Day – April 29**
  http://en.wikipedia.org/wiki/International_Dance_Day
- **Repeat Day – June 3**
  http://holidayinsights.com/other/repeatday.htm
- **Build-a-Scarecrow Day – First Sunday in July**
  http://holidayinsights.com/moreholidays/July/buildascarecrow.htm
- **International Chocolate Day – July 7**
  http://holidayinsights.com/other/chocolateday.htm
- **National Garage Sale Day – 2nd Saturday in August**
  http://festivals.ygoy.com/national-garage-sale-day/
- **International Lefthanders Day – August 13**
  http://www.lefthandersday.com/
- **Talk-Like-a-Pirate Day – September 19**
  http://talklikeapirate.com

- **Ask-a-Stupid-Question Day – September 28**
  http://www.holidayinsights.com/moreholidays/September/stupidquestionday.htm
- **False Confessions Day – November 21**
  http://www.holidayinsights.com/moreholidays/November/falseconfessionday.htm
- **Start-Your-Own-Country Day – November 22**
  http://www.theultimateholidaysite.com/holidays/2012-11/#!national-start-your-own-country-day
- **Festival-of-Enormous-Changes-at-the-Last-Minute – December 30**
  http://www.zanyholidays.com/2008/12/festival-of-enormous-changes-at-last.html

More Ways to Play

You don't need an entire day to work some play into the schedule. Here are a few ideas that take less than a full workday but that still bring light and life to the work routine.

Sing-Along

Kick off your day with a group sing-along. Energizing songs might chase away morning moodiness... or customers... or employees.

Leaving a Lasting Legacy Through Song

At the headquarters of a drug store in the Netherlands is a special ritual on Friday afternoons, where colleagues can play the music that they would want to have played at their funeral. It may sound bleak, but it's actually an uplifting and illuminating practice. Why? Because the song each person chooses is meaningful, embodying the essence of what he or she is all about. What a revealing thing to share, an act that immediately opens up others and allows them to feel safe being vulnerable as well.

Add 'Just a Spoonful of Humor' to your Meeting Agenda

To spice up your meeting, try adding a little play. For instance, you can add one-liners to the bottom of your agenda. A few that I've enjoyed: 'Life is like a dog sled ride: if you're not the lead dog, the scenery never changes.' 'Keep your words sweet; you never know when you may have to eat them.'

Another fun addition to an agenda might be a favorite dish from the last potluck. You may solve someone's 'what's for dinner tonight?' conundrum.

Consider including a quick opportunity for sharing, such as a one-minute opportunity to brag about your kids (choose an employee to do this pre meeting, or let everyone brag to their neighbor), or add in a few minutes to share some positive gossip about a co-worker (or yourself). These little diversions from the more relevant matters of the day can help establish a safe, positive, communal backdrop to the business at hand. Try one at your next meeting, and notice the increase in productivity that follows!

Company Picnics

A relaxing outdoor get-together can be a great connector when you add some activities. Eating together is already a great connecting opportunity, but doing it while sitting on a blanket on a beautiful green field makes it even better... well, that is if you're in love with your company.

One Minute, Many Laughs

My first book, *Using Humor for a Change*, highlights the 'one-minute humor break'. One way to define humor is that it is pain, embarrassment, or stress, distanced by time. What caused you stress last month, last year, or even three years ago, can make you laugh today. The question is, why do we have to wait to find the humor? Can't we access the humor and play as we're going through the pain? Now you can, with the help of the one-minute humor break. It's the ability to let go of the pain and choose to find the humor in the situation. It's a 'pattern interrupt' that changes our reactive stress pattern into one of play.

My favorite one-minute humor breaks:

Profanity With a Twist

Write a list of your favorite swear words on a piece of paper (some of you may need to use the back, or an entire notebook!). Then assign each word a number. The next time something upsets you, instead of screaming out the swear word, just scream out the number: '3, 13, 7!!!!!' 'Shove a 2 by 4 up your 8!' 'I've got your 265 right here.' This way, you can immediately release the stress, while the people around you wonder what those numbers mean. 'Don't get near Faisal, you know how he gets when he screams, "7!" Better stay away today.'

Sounds Like...

Another take on 'profanity with a twist' is to make up a word or phrase that sounds like the real deal. What does 'Sunny Beach – shut the front door,' sound like to you? You're almost guaranteed a good chuckle with yourself when using the 'sound-alike' swear words instead of the real ones. What sayings can you come up with that sound like the real thing?

Complain to ... Yourself!

Here's how it works: The next time you get angry about something, immediately pick up the phone, call your own home or your cell phone, and leave a message for yourself on your voicemail. 'Hi, Scott? This is Scott. If you're like me – and I think you are – we're not having a good day. The stock market is down 350 points again, my plane is delayed another three hours, and I'm going to be late on another deadline. My self-esteem is so low that even my imaginary friends won't play with me. No need to call me back; I'll just see you when you get home. And do me a favor and clean up the place a little, would you?' Once again, it's a quick way to release the stress, and you're sure to get a laugh out of the message when you check it later. Oh, and it's even more fun when you get the wrong number!

A Few Tips for Keeping Yourself in the Celebration

Reward Yourself

Make a game out of getting your work done. If you finish your paperwork in one hour without checking your wall on Facebook, treat yourself to a little something.

Associate the Bad With the Good

Pick the tasks you like the least, and spice 'em up with things you like the most. Most people don't like paperwork. Do you? Next time, while finishing your paperwork, indulge in things that you do enjoy. For instance, soft classical music, your favorite beverage, and some sweet chocolate will almost certainly make your paperwork more enjoyable.

One of my most tedious tasks is to send out 1000 New Year's postcards to my friends and clients outside of the US. So I do this each year while working in Thailand. (Postage and massages are both cheap there.) And how do I make it more enjoyable? I set myself up in a spa in Thailand with soothing music, a beverage, and a relaxing foot massage. I enlist any willing and available employee to help me put stamps on the cards. Then I give them a little gift for their efforts. I find this to be the perfect way to complete what would otherwise be a tedious task.

During this ritual, I also take time to reflect on being grateful for the clients and friends I'm addressing in the cards, as well as for the opportunity to do what I love. This is easy to do against the backdrop of a wonderful foot massage with tea and music.

Remember, you are often in control of the setting when you approach something you have to do. So why not make it more fun? You're allowed to play, too – and you'll be more likely to share that fun-loving spirit with others if you take care of yourself as well.

It's All in the Spirit

The spirit of play can work wonders in all areas of your life and help you bring out the best in yourself and others. If the culture of your organization embraces playfulness and encourages employees to have a good time while they're working – to joke, to laugh, to playfully tease one another – then you've increased your odds of creating a culture of celebration. As comedy writer Robert Orben puts it, 'If you can laugh together, you can work together.' And working together is the best recipe for long-term success.

ENDLESS SUPPLIES OF SURPRISE

Shhhh ... I think they are coming!

Everyone be quiet ... the door is opening ... on the count of three – ready? 1, 2, 3!

SURPRISE!!!

How much fun was that?

Every celebration can be enhanced with a little surprise. Surprise – it's all about adding an unexpected element of play. It's being in the state of play with the intent to trick or astonish others. If you want to keep a celebration fresh and fun, add a little surprise.

Not Your Average Holiday Party

Think back on your last holiday party, which is probably similar to many holiday parties hosted by organizations around the world. More than likely, this agenda will sound familiar: a chicken dinner followed by the annual company awards, after which a DJ plays music that's not so easy to dance to. And while you're there, you're also likely to be imagining ways you can fake your own death, right? Okay, maybe it's not that bad, but you get the idea ...

These are the times when the element of surprise is most welcome – and even necessary. It's a great opportunity to do something different, to shake it up a bit, to get your employees excited by a little novelty.

Back to the company holiday party: How about adding a little karaoke? Better yet, let the first few songs be sung by an Elvis impersonator who turns out to be your CEO, or by Frank, that lovable guy in accounting. All of a sudden there's a new energy, and people are ready to party!

You can make your awards more exciting, too, by coming up with a theme song customized for each recipient: *Born to be*

Wild, Bad to the Bone, Zippidy Doo-Dah. And why not go to the toy store and buy a little prop or gag gift to fit each honor? I'll bet Nate in marketing would love nothing more than a Slinky to show how flexible he is with ideas. Again, the goal is to create some excitement and laughter, and to keep your attendees wondering what's next.

Afternoon Surprise

A little surprise in the afternoon may be just what the Productivity Doctor ordered. To say 'thank you' upon the completion of a big project (or even in the middle of a project), or to break the monotony of working long hours, try an unexpected treat.

On the desk of a stressed employee, how about dropping off two movie passes for a new comedy in town? Or maybe tickets to an art exhibit, or a spa certificate for a massage? You could even bring in a massage therapist, reflexology specialist, or laughter facilitator. If you want to really (really!) surprise the gang, take them all out for margaritas at a local pub in the middle of the afternoon. You'll be surprised at the positive results of providing time for your employees to recharge their batteries. And you'll be making big deposits in their emotional bank accounts for making the effort.

Want to make the biggest impact? Customize it. Make sure that it's a surprise your employee will love by consulting with a spouse or close friends first. Then, sprinkle the surprise celebration with something high on this particular employee's joy list. Involve a son or daughter, provide a favorite food, include some favorite music.

Some organizations spend big money on a major event and showcase the honoree in front of the entire organization, only to find out later that he or she hates to be recognized in public. In most Asian countries, for instance, most employees prefer to be recognized as part of a team, rather than individually. The lesson here? Do your homework. If you don't, your plan could backfire (in which case the best surprise would have been no surprise). Try to let go of that self-absorbed mindset. Instead, come from a place of 'I want to create their WOW!' or 'How can I make them feel special?'

'The Platinum Rule' in Action

Surprise – or any kind of recognition – works best when you practice The Platinum Rule: Do onto others the way they want to be done unto.

I've been privileged to work with many wonderful companies, a large number of whom truly embrace a celebration mindset. However, none illustrates employee and customer surprise better than the Royal Plaza on Scotts, Singapore.

Mug Shot Surprise

Recently, Odette Huang, Director of Marketing and Branding at the Royal Plaza on Scotts, Singapore, asked her team to meet in the office on the fourth floor. No one knew why. Once they were all gathered, she went on: 'There comes a time in every life, or so you hope, when you find that special someone to share the rest of your days with.' Where was this going? 'Today, my assistant, Hooi Ching, is celebrating that leap into the unknown and is celebrating her sixth wedding anniversary. Oh but wait – there's more! Josephine and Joshua decided to take the leap on that exact same day (Josephine is another team member). Let's celebrate!'

Odette had created two nice coffee mugs with photos of the spouses on them, which she presented to each employee. Next, she had the team sing *Happy Anniversary*. It was a nice, quick, and touching celebration – one that didn't require much time, money, or effort. This quick surprise made two people feel special by acknowledging something good going on in their lives. You can bet that the rest of the workday was changed for the better because of these few moments.

Grab your Passport

Recently, at Royal Plaza on Scotts, Singapore, an employee who was promoted was set to be celebrated. Little did she know that her parents had been flown in from East Malaysia to Singapore to celebrate the promotion. At the ceremony, Odette Huang, VP of Marketing and Branding, turned to a team member and asked, 'Could you please grab that little wrapped gift on the second shelf in the closet next door?' Well, that 'little wrapped gift' turned out to be the employee's parents. Tears flowed freely, and the evening was all the more special for having shared such a meaningful surprise. Do you think the honoree will soon forget that ceremony?

Just Because...

At Royal Plaza staff meetings (routinely held after work hours), the management will often say, 'Today we're celebrating (you name it – it's Friday, it's been a long week, Anna closed a big sale), so we've prepared food for everyone, or we've brought in a special treat for everyone.' What a wonderful way to show your employees you care!

A Customer-Tailored Surprise

While you're at it, why not add the element of surprise into the lives of your customers? You may end up just as surprised when you realize how much fun it brings to your own life as well, not to mention the long-lasting connections you'll be forging.

Picture-Perfect

Nice touch-up ... thanks to help from Photoshop and a willing daughter.

When guests of the Royal Plaza book online, they are asked whether or not they are celebrating something special. One couple wrote that they were celebrating their fiftieth wedding anniversary. The Customer Relations team tracked down their daughter and got a wonderful photo from their wedding. Next, they used Photoshop to improve the picture quality and gave it an attractive frame.

Once the couple arrived, Odette invited them up to the Club Lounge together with the GM, Patrick Fiat, and the Customer Relation team. There, they sang *Happy Anniversary* and presented the framed photo to the astonished and teary-eyed couple. And why do you think they were in tears? Was the photo that bad? Did they feel depressed at how young they used to be? Of course not. They were deeply touched by the gesture, reminding us all of the old adage that a picture is worth a thousand tears – or rather, a thousand words.

Time for your Executive Check-Up

There's a client from New York who stays at the Royal Plaza once a year, every year. This guest mentioned that on his next visit he would be bringing his wife. Since he had been a loyal guest of the hotel for many years, Patrick, the GM, told him that he'd be given an executive suite ... or at least, that's what he'd meant to say. However, instead of saying 'executive suite', he said 'executive check-up' by mistake. Well, this became a running joke between Odette, Patrick, and the guest.

At 8:00 p.m ... one evening not long after this, the guest and his wife checked into their suite at the hotel. There, they found the guest's favorite Royal Plaza bread-and-butter pudding waiting for them. The next morning, there was a knock at their door. When the guest answered, he was greeted by Odette, Patrick, the doctor, and a lady from the front desk dressed up as a nurse, ready for the 'executive check-up'. The 'nurse' was even equipped with a stethoscope, a tongue depressor, and a thermometer – all from Fisher Price Toys. The clincher was a 'health certificate' with these results of the 'check-up': *Your symptoms include being a friendly, warm, loving, good-natured, caring, and all-around good guy. This clean bill of health will guarantee you many years of joy and laughter.* The guest (lovingly) replied that he would never again open the hotel door for anyone.

A Boxer a Day

When a returning guest at the Royal Plaza on Scotts, Singapore had been asked how his stay could have been made better, he mentioned that the laundry charges were too high. He claimed it would be cheaper to buy a new pair of underwear each day than to have them cleaned at the hotel.

In the bathroom, upon his arrival, was a new pair of silk boxer shorts for each day of the week. You can imagine what they might have looked like: Monday – a pair of smiley boxers, Tuesday – a banana character winking at you, Wednesday – Superman, Thursday – Cupid, draw back your bow ... you get the idea. What a nice surprise to feel good all under ... with an added smile for every day of the week. You can bet this customer won't be staying anywhere else after this unique and personal gesture!

The bottom (no pun intended) line is this: There are many ways to create greater customer connection through surprise. It may take a little longer to execute, but the payoff will be great in terms of customer loyalty, not to mention the satisfaction you'll feel from making someone's day – or stay!

Lesson learned? Add a little surprise into your relationships, and be ready for the returns of smiles, surprises, and more orders!

Planned Spontaneity

Ever wonder how comedians come up with just the right thing to say at just the right time? In a comedy club, a glass goes crashing to the floor. The comedian says, 'Just put that anywhere.'

One evening I was out watching another speaker with my good buddy Tim Gard, a fellow motivational humorist. In the middle of his talk, the guy fell right off the front of the stage. After making sure there was no blood, Tim turned to me and asked, 'What would you say right now if this had happened to you?' I thought for a moment and said, 'Don't mind me, it's just a stage I'm going through.' Not great, but not bad with three seconds notice. 'Tim, what would you say?' Tim smiled and said, 'I will now take questions ... from the floor.'

That, my friend, is a good example of *planned spontaneity* – a form of surprise that makes work and life more fun for all parties involved. And it's so much better than not saying anything at all, which was unfortunately the (non)response of the stunned speaker that day.

A Quip a Day Keeps the Doldrums Away

Work can get repetitive and monotonous, and it's easy to become disengaged. We can keep it fresh and interesting by coming up with new lines to the questions we hear every day.

For instance, when checking in at the airport and the lady at the counter says, 'Mr Friedman, your final destination?' maybe I'd say, 'Hopefully Heaven, but today I'm only going to Jakarta.'

From a potential client who calls and asks, 'Can I get a quote over the phone?' I might answer, 'Sure; here you go: "The road to wisdom is long and hard, so wear comfortable shoes." Care for another quote?'

Or how about those times when someone calls you the wrong name?

'Hi Steve!'

'It used to be Steve, but I changed it to Scott last Tuesday.'

The conversation that follows is always a lot of fun ...

And let's not forget those off-hand times when we have the opportunity to surprise someone with an unexpected quip. Consider the time when you're at dinner party at someone's house, and you're in the toilet. Someone out in the hallway turns the handle of the door, only to find it locked. Normally, you would say, 'I'm in here; be out in a minute.' Next time, try, 'Come in! I've been waitinggggg!' Now there's a way to spice up any dinner party!

One of my favorite examples of planned spontaneity comes from my good friend and motivational speaker, W. Mitchell, who happens to be a paraplegic confined to a wheelchair. When he wheels up to the plane and the flight attendant asks, 'Can you walk to your seat from here?' he responds, 'I can, but I only have a few steps left, and I didn't want to use them up today.'

What a nice way to build connection without leaving the other person feeling bad about their remark. That's the outcome we're going for. Connect, engage, make it fun for them – and let your efforts make it even more fun for you!

It's Up to You, It's Up to Me

After all these tips and examples, you may be wondering who is responsible for the surprise? The answer is (triply) simple: somebody, anybody, everybody. Consider creating a 'celebration committee' (more on this next chapter) whose task is to keep celebrations fresh and inspiring. A rotating 'VP of Surprise' or 'Champion of Fun' can get it all started. The key is to continually shake it up, move it forward, and keep your employees excitedly anticipating what amazing experience might happen next.

Summary

Can you feel that celebration mindset taking hold yet? Good. Then you have officially turned on your GPS. Now, how do we keep it running?

- Start by making a commitment to facing each moment of the day with as much **Gratitude**, **Playfulness**, and **Surprise** as you can muster. Staying in the spirit of play as much as possible (as in '**G**o **P**lay **S**ome') will help you let go of worry, anxiety, and pressure. Your GPS will help you embrace the positive emotions of curiosity, spontaneity, passion, joy, and love for all you do.

- **Remember, each of us has a choice at how we look at things.** We can mope in the rain, or we can be thankful for the gift of moisture and carry a bright yellow, polka-dot umbrella. Practice gratitude, and you will forever enrich your life.

When you operate with your GPS turned to 'on', something good is bound to happen. In other words, life can make you bitter, or life can make you better. Choose better; choose GPS. And let's keep the celebration going!

Chapter 3 Why Celebrate?

Now that your GPS is on, it's time to Celebrate! (Or, as Kool and the Gang put it, 'CELEBRATE GOOD TIMES – COME ON!')

A whopping 87 per cent of our survey respondents believe that celebrating success is important. Interestingly, over 80 per cent also admitted that they don't celebrate enough.

The truth is, far too many people have amazing lives that go uncelebrated. They don't celebrate success at work, and they don't celebrate often (if at all) at home. They simply live their lives, completing one task or project after the next. Chances are, it's because they've never defined what success looks like. They haven't turned on their GPS. Well, I'm going to assume that your GPS is now turned on and ready to go. And in that spirit, let's move on to begin to define success.

THE MANY FACES – AND PHASES – OF SUCCESS

Whether personal or career-related, big or small, success must be broken into small, measurable increments. This way, it becomes much easier both to acknowledge and to celebrate.

So how do we break down success into smaller strides worth celebrating? Let's say your goal is to lose ten kilos in five weeks. That breaks down into two kilos per week. Why not celebrate every day you've spent eating the right foods, exercising, and taking responsibility for your health? If you miss the target on one of the weeks, you can still celebrate by making new choices around lessons learned while falling short of your objectives. And of course, when you do lose that two kilos for the week, a celebration is in order!

The same applies to any project in the workplace. Let's take a common task, such as completing the company budget with a two-week deadline. Begin by breaking down what needs to happen on a day-to-day, week-to-week basis. That way, you can celebrate those 'success milestones' along the way.

For instance, when you finish the first milestone, take the team to lunch. For the next, surprise them with lattes to start off a meeting. Another milestone might lead to a clever song or cheer (written by the Celebration Committee or another musically-inclined employee). And finally, when the budget is finished, a celebratory breakfast can be shared by all.

When you run into challenges or need to make changes along the way, celebrate each new beginning, along with the growth that comes from setbacks. By acknowledging what went right *and* wrong, you instill a sense of value to every step of the journey ... and knowing the value of our efforts is truly a cause for celebration in itself!

Training for Celebration

How might we break down and celebrate the increments of success while implementing a new training program?

Your first step – or milestone – might be to form a project team. Make it a celebration, and consider investing in a t-shirt for everyone involved (or another item that symbolizes everyone's ownership in the project).

For the next milestone, or Step 2, call a meeting to design the timeline and the plan. From there, you can even send out 'teasers' hinting at what is coming. A little teaser gift connected to the big launch will go a long way among your employees to stir up even more excitement!

Step 3 will come down the road – say, a few months later. Why not host a quiz (or even a mock quiz show) relating to all the information you want employees to know about the big launch? And for more celebration, offer gifts to the quiz winners – thumb drives or the latest tech gadgets, colorful mugs with the company logo, or post-it pads with metallic pens – the options are endless.

Then, when the big launch comes, it's time for the major celebration! Why not go all out with posters around the office, cotton candy and popcorn machines, carnival games, and a nice buffet lunch? Then you can ho d a ribbon-cutting ceremony featuring a talk from the president or team leader.

No doubt you will discover that the motivation to keep this and other projects going successfully will likely stay high. Why? Because those simple, micro-celebrations along the way – not to mention the big launch itself – will have your employees interested, invested, and on-target.

So there you have it: one illustration of how to set yourself up for success! No need to create a definition of success around an insurmountable task. Break it down, and applaud each step. As our survey shows, it's important – and remarkably easy – to pay attention to our successes in life. As for your investment in time and energy, just a little of both will yield big dividends.

So keep on that GPS, and make it easy to celebrate!

The Finish Line

JoAnna Brandi, customer care and positive leadership coach (www.returnonhappiness.com), has some valuable advice on how to acknowledge the good in our lives.

Sometimes we can do this just by changing our language and our 'frame' on things. For instance, change the word 'deadline' to 'finish line'. 'Deadline' is too dramatic and implies somebody could get hurt: *If you don't get this project done by Monday, there are going to be some dead bodies ...* or *We met the deadline, but we lost two people in the process.* This sort of doomsday-type thinking can't be good for the workplace!

On the other hand, 'finish line' says, *Hey! Here we come, we're close, it's time to get ready for a celebration!* The cheerleaders are jumping up and down, the crowd is going wild, Rajen in Accounting just pulled out his French horn ... yes, it's going to be a party! Every small milestone that you set for yourself should have its own finish line (not to mention its own cheerleaders, even if that's just you with a couple of pompoms!).

THE 'MICRO-CELEBRATION': SMALL EFFORTS, BIG RESULTS

Many people we talked to were concerned that if you celebrate too often, the value of celebration might become diluted.

This is a valid concern; however, not every celebration needs champagne and a party. Small milestones can be acknowledged with snacks, songs, cheers, pats on the back, or just a few simple, but meaningful, words. The micro-celebration will keep your team engaged and connected, which in turn will help build momentum until a project is complete.

Remember the saying, 'Great things often come in small packages'? Well, the micro-celebration is proof of this. Test it for yourself, and watch how things begin to change for you and your colleagues!

A Word is Worth a Thousand Smiles

Remember as kids when we had a secret code word to give us entrance into the club? Everyone wanted to know the special word, because everyone wanted to belong.

Having a 'celebration word' is kind of like that. The word can be our own secret code word, or it can be shared by a department to acknowledge a job well done. The word can be used in memos, emails, and personal notes. It can also be mentioned in meetings, while passing a hard-working colleague at the copy center, or as passage to get you on the elevator. And changing your celebration word every few months will help keep things fresh.

Here are some of my favorite celebration words: *Fantastico, Bravo, Woo-hoo, YES!, Hooray, Zippidy Doo Dah, All right!* And, if you really want to make them come alive, add a little action, too. You can do silly motions such as these: hands over head in a 'V' for victory, fist pump, shake your booty ... you get the picture. Now go ahead – think creatively to come up with some of your own!

A Song and Dance

Music is a simple, inexpensive way to celebrate, change your emotional state, and bring people together. As U2's Bono said, 'Music can change the world, because it can change people.' For this reason, incorporating music into your celebration toolkit makes a lot of sense. Below are a few illustrations of how music can turn an ordinary day or event into something spectacular.

Personal Theme Songs

Why not micro-celebrate now to the tune of your own personal theme song? You can 'borrow' a song from a favorite recording artist or television show, or you can adapt the words from a children's song, Christmas carol, the theatre, or (if you're daring enough!) even your favorite superhero.

Here are a few examples of personal theme songs that participants have sung to me in recent programs:

Mighty Mouse

Mr. Trouble never hangs around

When he hears this Mighty sound:

Here I come to save the day!

That means that Mighty Mouse is on the way!

Yes sir, when there is a wrong to right

Mighty Mouse will join the fight!

On the sea or on the land

He's got the situation well in hand!

My favorite was from a Chinese Singaporean, sung in a program I conducted in Singapore recently:

> *Oh Lord it's hard to be humble*
>
> *When you're perfect in every way.*
>
> *I can't wait to look in the mirror*
>
> *'Cuz I get better-looking each day*
>
> *To know me is to love me*
>
> *I must be a hell of a man.*
>
> *Oh Lord it's hard to be humble*
>
> *But I'm doing the best that I can.*
>
> *(Written by Mac Davis; lyrics from www.lyricsmode.com)*

Now it's your turn. What would be your song? I challenge you to find one, or even to write one of your own. And, if necessary to go along with the song, feel free to go out and buy a cape!

A Song for Every Occasion

Along with *Celebrate* by Kool and the Gang, included in the following list are 50 inspiring, uplifting songs. Consider playing a few at your next celebration, use one as the focal piece for a micro-celebration, or just tune into one when you need a little inspiration. There are hundreds, even thousands, more out there – so go ahead and add a few of your own to make the list complete!

1) *When You Believe* – Mariah Carey & Whitney Houston
2) *You Raise Me Up* – Josh Groban
3) *Power of Dreams* – Celine Dion
4) *Go the Distance* – Michael Bolton
5) *One Moment in Time* – Whitney Houston
6) *I Gotta Feeling* – Black Eyed Peas
7) *I Just Want to Celebrate* – Rare Earth
8) *Don't Stop Believin'* – Journey
9) *Hero* – Mariah Carey
10) *Stronger* – Britney Spears
11) *I Will Survive* – Gloria Gainer
12) Theme from *Rocky (Gonna Fly Now)*
13) *Just the Way You Are* – Bruno Mars
14) *Firework* – Katy Perry
15) *Born this Way* – Lady Gaga
16) *I Want to Hold Your Hand* – Glee (original song by the Beatles)
17) *One of Us* – Glee (original song by Joan Osborne)
18) *So Beautiful or So What* – Paul Simon
19) *Zippidy Doo Dah* – Disney
20) *Dare You to Move* – Switchfoot

21) *Everyone is No. 1* – Andy Lau

22) *I Believe I can Fly* – R. Kelly

23) *Wind Beneath my Wings* – Bette Midler

24) *We Will Rock You* – Queen

25) *All the Good* – Jana Stanfield

26) *If I Were Brave* – Jana Stanfield

27) *The Trick is to Learn to Enjoy the Ride* – Jana Stanfield

28) *Eye of the Tiger* – Survivor

29) *Somewhere Over the Rainbow* – Israel Kamakawiwo'ole (originally by Judy Garland)

30) *The Climb* – Miley Cyrus

31) *Walking on Sunshine* – Katrina & the Waves

32) *Beautiful Sunday* – Daniel Boone

33) *Simply the Best* – Tina Turner

34) *There Must Be an Angel (Playing With My Heart)* – Eurythmics

35) *What a Wonderful World* – Louis Armstrong

36) *Reach* – Gloria Estefan

37) *Dare You to Move* – Switchoot

38) *Never Surrender* – Corey Hart

39) *You Gotta Want It* – Roberta Gold

40) *Win* – Brian McKnight

41) *Heal the World* – Michael Jackson

42) *When you Believe* – Mariah Carey, Whitney Houston

43) *Chariots of Fire* – Vangelis

44) *It's my Life* – Bon Jovi

45) *Return to Innocence* – Enigma

46) *Beautiful Day* – U2

47) *Live Like You Were Dying* – Tim McGraw

48) *I Feel Good* – James Brown

49) *We Are the Champions* – Queen

50) *A New Day Has Come* – Celine Dion

Categorize your songs on your digital player for different desired states of mind. With intention and the right music, it's amazing how you can change the mood, the meeting, the gathering ... even the entire day.

Victory Dance

What does most every athlete have that we need? A victory dance! Dance, like music, helps us unwind, smile, and connect. It's 'shaking your booty' in whatever way feels good. Do your favorite aerobics move, twist and shout, shake your pelvis just like Elvis. Get the accounting department out of their seats for an impromptu boogie to celebrate a milestone, or serve some disco with your morning meeting (it goes well with coffee!). A victory dance is the perfect micro-celebration!

Hokey Pokey Your Success

How about a 'Hokey Pokey' moment? Send a quick instant message or announcement to all employees, asking them to meet in the conference room, lobby, or other spacious room. Imagine their faces when, once they arrive, they are asked to form a circle as you play the 'Hokey Pokey' song! And from there, it goes something like this:

'You put you right foot in, you put your right foot out, you put your right foot in, and you shake it all about. You do the Hokey Pokey and you turn yourself around, that's what it's all about!'

There's no question that one simple, silly song and dance will be likely to change someone's morning (including yours). It's a perfect, three-minute way to take a break and celebrate the success of the moment. And just think of all the fun your employees will have later, when they tell their friends and family about the impromptu laugh they had at work that day!

CELEBRATING SUCCESS WEEKLY: COMPLETION, DELETION, CREATION, AND SOUL FOOD

In ***The Joy of Success***, author Susan Ford Collins shares her years of extensive research on success. She breaks down the characteristics of the most successful people into three areas: *Completion, Deletion,* and *Creation*. JoAnna Brandi also uses these three points as a weekly ritual, with an additional one of her own, *Soul Food*. As JoAnna explains, we can spend every waking moment working if we want to, but without 'Soul Food' our lives will be empty. Therefore we need to take time out for what really matters. Every Friday – hopefully with a glass of wine or sparkling cider – JoAnna celebrates her week in review based on these elements of success.

Let's take a closer look at each one:

Completion

What have you achieved this week? What have you completed? Closing an important project at work, settling a misunderstanding with your spouse or boss, finishing the budget (or a painting or a puzzle, for that matter), completing part one of a new project, retiring a policy or a person, or even making a big mistake at a meeting and then sharing the lesson are all accomplishments worth noting and, yes, celebrating!

Deletion

What did you get rid of this week of that no longer serves you? As Peter Drucker once said, 'Most managers know what to do, but what they don't know is what to stop doing.' What do you need to stop doing? What could you delegate or cut out altogether?

So as you review your own life, consider your own recent 'deletions'. Did you clean out your office, a drawer, or a filing cabinet? Is there a toxic relationship you finally said 'Adios' to? And what items did you replace or update around the house and office? We need to get rid of the old to make room for the new.

Creation

What have you created this week? A new project? New connections, or old connections renewed? A newer and better recipe, a trip for business or pleasure, a committee devoted to celebrations in the workplace? Or maybe you've made just a few simple, minor changes – such as dyeing your hair orange, buying a mini-bus, and moving to Miami ...

Big or small, major or minor, you must have created something. And something is always worth celebrating!

Soul Food

And finally, what did you do that fed your soul? How would you like to spend your time if you could do anything? Yoga? Yoda? Meditation? Healthy eating? Vitamins, or a body cleanse? A walk on the beach with a good friend? Family time? Soul-full reading?

What did you do this week along these lines? What are your favorite memories of the week? Reward yourself for honoring the 'soul food' in your life with a little more soul food.

Pamper Thyself

Recharging while away from work helps us all bring our best back to the world. Don't forget to do nice things for yourself, and encourage your colleagues to do the same. The result will be a better-rested, happier, and more productive you.

Here are a few ways to bring a little self-celebratory soul food to your life:

- Buy yourself a gift, such as a nice pair of shoes, the newest techno gadget, eyewear, or some gourmet ice cream.
- Take yourself out to a favorite restaurant, or visit a nice spa for a massage or a treatment. If you crave some local adventure, get yourself tickets to a sporting event, the theatre or opera, a ballet or a musical. For a spur-of-the-moment change of scenery, consider a brisk walk in the park, a class at the fitness center, or a leisurely stroll through the museum.

You might be asking, *But how can the soul food concept help me in the workplace?* The answers may surprise you. Bringing in our favorites is the perfect way to help celebrate our micro-successes!

There are many tried-and-true ways to add a little 'soul food' to any work environment:

Food for Thought

For instance, one universal favorite that's sure to appeal to everyone's spirit is through FOOD. Your favorite snack – or that of your colleagues – is always a welcome celebration! Who wouldn't feel a sense of celebration when, at an afternoon meeting, banana-fudge sundaes are served with the agenda?

The Play's the Thing

Let's be honest: Aren't we all just oversized children at times? This can be a good thing, especially when it comes to micro-celebrations. For a little added fun in or out of the workplace, play a kazoo, a nose flute, or any other hand-crafted instrument made out of objects around the office. Make some rhythm with a plastic hand clapper, do a cheer in the mirror, go shopping online, or call a friend ... then snack some more. And don't forget to take photos of the celebration to share with office mates or to post on your Facebook. Why not spread the fun and create some soul food for others?

MICRO-CELEBRATIONS TO ACKNOWLEDGE OTHERS

As you've seen throughout this chapter, remembering the little things is a wonderful way to change someone's work experience for the better. And a better day can lead to a better week, month, and year for everyone.

Recognition

Your staff members make a great effort to get their work done and help your company grow. Shouldn't they be recognized accordingly?

The most common ways to show appreciation are personal thank-yous (in person or in notes), compliments, pats on the back, or public recognition. Any of these are small gestures – so easy to do, yet so powerful! But there are more ways out there too. Here are a few to get your wheels turning:

Online Rewards

The Australian software company Atlassian has a 'kudos' system which allows anyone in the organization the opportunity to give credits/kudos/points to another colleague for a job well done. The recognized colleague gets a thank-you note on behalf of the company that is then posted to the internal network for all to see. With 'points' earned this way, employees can purchase goods from an online store. According to the Global HR Chief, Joris Luijke, having an organizational venue for compliments has proven to be a great motivator for all employees.

If you try this, consider posting the kudos in a prominent space in the office as well. This little gesture will further emphasize the praise for those hard-working employees.

Overdose of Appreciation

Hewlett-Packard has created a special 'Appreciation Day' for exceptional employees. On this day, outstanding staff members are recognized every fifteen minutes for eight hours straight, with songs, cards, notes, and other fun gifts.

The jewelry and accessory store Claire's rewards their district managers every Saturday with a traveling trophy filled with gifts.

You can find or create all sorts of 'awards' to grace employees in your office all year long. Here are a few more ideas from others in our research:

- Leave a bouquet of flowers on an outstanding employee's desk
- 'Caught-in-the-Act-of-Kindness' prizes
- 'SMILE Awards' for positive people

Poster Boy

Great performers at Honeywell are recognized by getting their 'G' (an insignia meaning 'great performer'). Recipients are photographed to appear on motivational posters hung throughout the office.

MAKING THE MOST OF THE MICRO

As we've seen, micro-celebrations are a wonderful way of acknowledging the small successes accomplished by you or your team along the way. At the same time, there are some factors to consider in determining whether your micro-celebrations are having the desired impact on the ones you want to honor.

Sage Advice

Chester Elton offers us excellent guidelines on how to appreciate other people: *Do it frequently, be specific, and do it right after he or she does something good. If you fall short in any of these three areas, your compliment or appreciation might come off as being less meaningful or sincere.*

What, So What, Now What?

To make the greatest impact with your praise and recognition, practice what Rick Rios does in Anchorage, Alaska, at community leadership luncheons. Whenever he praises someone, he uses the 'What, So What and Now What?' principle he learned from his friend Chad Starkle:

What – Specifically, what did you like? What did you learn?

So What – Who are the people and/or things impacted by what you did?

Now What? – How will your actions impact the future? Helping the people you recognize see a bigger picture of what they do – and have accomplished – will surely inspire them to do even more. This attention to the essence of their action is a sure way to make them feel authentically appreciated.

Remember, It Really is the Little Things...

One of the nicest gifts you can give someone is your appreciation. Make your gesture special in these ways:

- Customize your attention for each individual employee. The highest form of appreciation is personal. Who wouldn't want to find a surprise breakfast at the office courtesy of a manager, complete with a sincere expression of appreciation? And wouldn't any of us feel special being honored with a poem or a song composed just for us?

- Add a handwritten personal note with specific praise. Listing reasons or ways in which someone is appreciated is best of all, as it shows you are paying attention to both the work and the person.

FROM MICRO TO MACRO

Some companies do an outstanding job in celebrating small successes with micro-celebrations, which in turn lead to larger and more all-inclusive events. One such company from our research is The SCOOTER Store in the United States.

A Bang! to Let the Games Begin

The SCOOTER Store keeps cans of confetti available throughout the building to shower unsuspecting employees in a spontaneous celebration at any given moment. It might be sprinkled on an employee who experienced a life event, or on another who had a best personal month.

But the celebrating isn't just for personal triumphs; it's also for team accomplishments. Each month, teams get together to celebrate accomplishments reached in the previous month. Often, they arrange fun-filled competitions against other teams in their division. The winning team gets to be 'served' by the other team – either with fresh-cooked omelets, pancakes, or even car washes. Sometimes the stakes are set higher, with bosses ending up with their heads shaved or dyed blue. Or, to celebrate summer goal winners, a team will occasionally get to wear shorts and caps to work for the day (blue hair optional!). And, along the way, some teams will have a balloon pop-off as a visual way to show goals being accomplished.

Team celebrations are among the most popular and recurring ways The SCOOTER Store celebrates their successes.

POP This!

To be most effective, celebrations must include everyone. Here's one celebration that makes it possible for everybody to play, every month:

Right Selection in Dubai organizes seminars and training programs, and also distributes great books. They keep their staff motivated with a process costing only pennies. Gautam Ganglani, General Manager, writes:

> *At the beginning of the month, we distribute six colorful balloons to each staff member in the office. Each time any staff member receives good news – over the phone, fax, or email – he or she blows up a balloon and pops it with a loud bang. Everyone notices and asks what the good news is, which then spreads quickly throughout the office. The first person to burst all six balloons each month wins dinner for two at a restaurant. Then we restart the process with six new balloons each and another free dinner to be won.*

This creates a lot of anticipation for good news, followed by excitement and communication each time someone bursts a balloon.

Good news in our case is qualified and quantified by sales of a minimum amount, a contract confirmed, a client calling to thank us for spectacular service, registration of a large group, or confirmation of event sponsors.

We have been bursting quite a few balloons lately, creating excitement from each person's eagerness to create more frequent positive results!

Bang! Another winner!

1001 Ways

In the book *1001 Ways to Reward Employees,* Bob Nelson gives some great ideas on how to celebrate success. Thanks Bob, for permission to use a few:

Hello? It's Your Motivation Calling!

The company Business First sends out daily voicemail messages to all employees, each with a joke, a success story, or a motivational message. So, as an employee, you just never know what will show up on that voicemail! I think this idea is doubly helpful if the message is inspiring and can be kept as a source of motivation during tough moments in a project.

Imagine Monday afternoon at 3 p.m. The weekend is further away than ever, and you feel stuck in your project. Wouldn't a great message from your supervisor showing support and confidence in your abilities do wonders to help you to recharge? Wouldn't this small gesture ease your mind and give you the 'push' to tackle the problem once again? Of course it would!

Pause For Applause

Here's another great idea: At Doolittle & Burroughs, the management team sent out an email to all staff asking everyone to stop and applaud at exactly 4 p.m. This gesture was a way to honor all service departments in the company for the great progress they were making. Micro-celebration at its finest!

Chew On Your Success

The company Chilton Ellet has a unique way to celebrate small successes. They give a penny to an employee for every three deals that employee closes. The penny is dropped into a gumball machine, and the employee gets paid a pre-set amount based on the color of the gumball: 25 cents, $3 or $10. What a great and fun way to reward your employees!

Care for a Car Wash With That?

The Resident Home Company gives their employees free car washes on location on payday Friday. How nice to bring home your paycheck in a shiny new car! 'Honey, put on your best dress! We're going out this evening!'

And the Celebration Continues...

Our own research has led us to find even more excellent, creative ways to celebrate in the workplace. Below are a few of our favorites.

Talking to a Wall

Ever feel like you're talking – or walking – into a wall? Surely it's not a problem when the wall is made of cards, with each card describing how your colleagues and supervisors appreciate you, your effort, and all the joy you bring to the organization.

Smile and Share Some Love

Set up a camera and a microphone in a spare office or conference room that is open for everybody. Invite any or all employees to go in and record a message expressing appreciation for a colleague. The resulting film can be used to kick off a meeting, to lend a personal flavor to the company video, or even as a marketing tool to show potential employees or clients what a special company you are.

A Cubicle of Epic Decorations

Transform an honored employee's cubicle into a personalized celebratory scene. How?

- Highlight it with the person's favorite color.
- Create a landscape with toy trains, ping-pong paddles, or favorite hobby items.

- Fill the entire cubicle with the employee's favorite snacks.
- Fill the cubicle with table tennis balls and ping-pong paddles.
- Cover the space with different colors of paper or post-it notes.
- Put the Starbucks logo everywhere.
- Turn the cubicle into a ski resort.

My Bucket Runneth Over

Here's an original idea shared by a school, but applicable in any work environment. Each teacher has a bucket with their name on it. The goal is to keep everyone's buckets filled. Anyone can add to another's bucket with notes, little gifts, photos, candy, etc. In this way, everyone is validated and nourished by the give-and-take of keeping those buckets full. At the same school, parents are also able to get in on the metaphorical 'bucket filling' by regularly preparing lunch for the teachers to show their appreciation.

One Size (or Style) Does Not Fit All

We've seen a wide array of micro-celebrations, from dances to hand-written notes to songs, games, and speeches. These are all wonderful and help commemorate the moment. Through our research, we found many other ways to show appreciation. These include material gifts such as gift cards, movie tickets, theatre tickets, amusement park passes, a night out to a casino, dinner in a nice restaurant, even a ski holiday. So what's with these bigger gifts, and how do we determine which times call for such a gesture?

The bottom line is this: Bigger celebrations for bigger occasions. It is that simple!

There should be a nice balance between honoring both the honoree and the rituals of the company. When planning gifts, consider things people value most. Often, these things aren't 'things' at all! For instance, everyone appreciates learning opportunities, especially when they involve travel to cool places. Humanitarian trips, stock options, and sporting and community events are also favorites.

And if your employees don't qualify for the big gifts, creativity makes up for a lot. Here are a few examples of low-cost, unique celebrations for you to try on:

Dump a Dog

Finish a project, and you're rewarded with the chance to 'dump a dog'. No, this doesn't mean you're tossing Fido out in the harsh desert. It does, however, mean you can pass the thing you like the least to your manager, who then assigns it to another employee. (Hopefully this next employee will finish quickly as well, so the 'dumping' can make fair rounds.)

Buy Your Boss

Great Western, during their appreciation banquet, auctions off services to be performed by upper management. Each employee is given $200 to bid on car washings, babysitting, meal-making, or taking over an employee's job for six hours.

Me, on a Menu? (from **1001 Ways***)*

That's right – at Wells Fargo Bank, when you win 'employee of the month', a cafeteria item will be named after you. Hmm, what would you want to be? I'll take the KFC Scott Fried-man bucket of chicken, please.

So what shall it be: micro or macro celebration? You make the call. As long as every deadline is a finish line, you'll be smiling all along the way.

Yes, You CAN Celebrate!

I know, I know – saying that you're going to plan a celebration is much easier (or so you think) than making it happen. Well, what if I told you that it all is much more feasible than you may think?

Sure, there are logistical details to consider in planning a celebration, just as there would be for any other company event. But if you look at the big picture – and at the outcome it will manifest – you'll see that making a celebration happen is almost as easy (and doubly as magical) as clicking together those ruby slippers and saying, 'There's no place like here, there's no time like now ...'

Here, a few considerations, and a bit of advice to ease the way:

The Economics of Celebration: Small Investment, Big Payoff

So what about funding, you may ask?

A celebration from the heart without spending any money can be wildly successful. However, at some point, there are likely to be some costs involved. Given the enormous impact of celebration on engagement and performance, a celebration budget makes good sense.

Even more good news: there are many ways to fund celebrations – from the HR budget, to payroll deductions, to creative celebration fundraisers. (And these fundraisers can be celebrations in themselves!)

Therefore, don't let money deter your celebration efforts. Creativity and care will make up for an expensive celebration. And if you need to put off a big event, start small and enjoy the micro-celebrations along the way!

The Celebration Committee

Many organizations we interviewed have created a committee that helps guide celebrations. Whether driven by the CEO, Director of HR or a front-line employee, the committee should have everyone on board before you start. Your ideal candidates for a celebration committee will be social, caring, loving, enthusiastic, energetic, fun, playful, culturally sensitive, and (most importantly!) excited about planning celebrations. Of course, you'll need a few solid follow-up people as well. It's best to rotate committee members so that you avoid burnout while keeping the ideas fresh. Come up with a yearly plan, and always remain open to a little spontaneity.

Inviting Celebration With Style

Keep in mind, too, that the way you set up a celebration event can be as important as the celebration itself. A clever invitation, a surprise gift, a colorful, festive electronic invitation with music – such pre-details set the expectation that this is a party not to miss. And make sure you have a few champions of celebration that help spread the word in an enthusiastic way!

HONORING MISTAKES

The celebration with the biggest pay-off may very well be the celebration of mistakes. You don't get success without failure, so why not appreciate the valuable lessons? After all, we learn far more from our failures than we do from our successes. My favorite definition of success is 'moving from failure to failure with enthusiasm'.

That's why the concept of a 'no-blame' culture is found in many of the world's most admired organizations. Instead of placing blame on someone or something else when things go wrong, the focus shifts to the lesson.

So what's to learn? We can start with this: How can we best make changes and new choices based on the lessons gained from this experience? Even the language we use to describe setbacks should reflect this attitude. For instance, in your organization, why not change the words 'mistake' and 'failure' to 'lessons learned' or 'wisdom gained'?

The Power of Risk

According to a survey from the 2010 World HRD Congress in Mumbai, the #1 killer of innovation is having a culture that hesitates to empower employees to take risks.

In other words, if we encourage our employees to go on and take those calculated risks, we will get more creative, pioneering solutions. And by encouraging everyone to celebrate lessons learned from setbacks, there will be no need for anyone to cover up or shrink from their mistakes. Sharing one another's setbacks will become an indispensable teaching tool for moving the entire company forward.

Losing into Winning

There's no questioning the value of learning from mistakes. But is it possible to go a step further, and bring light and fun to them as well? We came across some clever awards in honoring mistakes:

- 'Golden Lemon of the Year' award is ProTeas Hotel's annual prize for the biggest mistake. Even the CEO won the award one year, which now makes it more acceptable to be the recipient. The award encourages transparency, honesty, and learning from mistakes.

- A funny bobble-head doll is earned by an event administrator to symbolize the gratitude of the facility. For what, you ask? For not being struck by lightning when everything that could go wrong, did!
- 'Biggest Booboo Award' – One company gives a box of Band-Aids when mistakes are made, to put over the 'booboo'. When you get the Band-Aids, you have to share the lesson.

A Lesson and a Smile...

Whatever the award may be, the point is to learn from a mistake and to bring a sense of fun to it as well. In a supportive and encouraging culture, the experiences shared are not only useful; they are also frequently humorous and entertaining – resulting in an increase in trust, openness, and creativity.

$50 for the Best Mistake

A sales manager slept through her alarm and missed a flight, along with an important meeting with a customer. At the next sales meeting, she pulled out a $50 bill and placed it on the conference table. She then shared what had happened as well as the lesson gained. Next, she challenged all of her salespeople to share a mistake they had made in the past month, and what they'd learned. The person who had the biggest mistake with the best lesson learned was awarded the $50. This became a monthly ritual, leading to more transparency and a more authentically connected team.

Hungry for Mistakes

At a recent program of mine in Karachi, Pakistan, Sr Executive Parveen Hatim (Shares Department) of Pakistan State Oil (PSO) relayed another excellent example of celebrating mistakes. There, the person who makes the mistake is responsible for providing delicious, healthy snacks (samosas, sandwiches, patties, rolls, etc.) for the entire department. Anyone in the department is allowed to identify the mistake – be it the manager while signing the order, or any colleague who happens to spot an error in a price comparative, or in processing or procedures. It's a subtle and beneficial way to understand the repercussions of a mistake, while hopefully helping to avoid a repeat of the error. According to Parveen, people actually look forward to the occasional mistakes made in the office because of the food that inevitably follows. Unfortunately for the hungry hopefuls (but fortunately for the company), mistakes have been reduced in part through this tradition.

Don't Say or Pay! (as told by Rhonda Faught)

'Bill Richardson was elected Governor of the State of New Mexico in November 2002 and took office in January 2003. He appointed me to head the Highway Department. Governor Richardson made it clear that he wanted the Department to about be more than highways. He wanted us to have a commuter rail, statewide transit facilities, and be more bicycle friendly ... he wanted a multimodal Department of Transportation.

'One of the first pieces of legislation passed in Governor Richardson's administration changed our name from the New Mexico State Highway and Transportation Department (NMSHTD – hated that acronym) to the New Mexico Department of Transportation (NMDOT). The law took effect on July 1, 2003.

'In preparation for this major change, we had a multimodal transportation summit in Albuquerque, where we invited DOT employees and stakeholders from across the state. It was then that I decided to charge a dollar to each person who said 'Highway Department".

'At the end of the two-and-a-half day conference, Governor Richardson addressed the attendees with the press present from all the TV stations and area newspapers. He began with, 'It's so good to see so many people from the Highway Department here today. Well, I just named the new Highway Commission today ...' I couldn't stand it, so I took the microphone away from the Governor and said, "Governor, we are NOT the 'Highway Department' any more. We are a multimodal 'Department of Transportation' – and for that I have to charge you a dollar.' The two hundred plus people in attendance were looking at me thinking: this lady is either really stupid or very courageous. The governor reached into his wallet and pulled out a dollar bill. Then he started talking, and darn if he didn't say 'Highway Department' again! Once again, he pulled out his wallet and handed me a dollar bill. The crowd cheered. Then, for the third time, the governor said "Highway Department". This time he turned to me and said, "I don't have another dollar bill." Everyone in the room went crazy, and people

were pulling out their wallets waving dollar bills in the air saying, "I have one!" I collected $166 that day.

The headlines the next day said, "Transportation Secretary Fines Governor a Dollar for Saying 'Highway Department.'" I had that article framed with three dollar bills and gave it to him as a gift a few days later.

'This was just the beginning. EVERYONE now knew that were a multimodal Department of Transportation – we didn't just build highways, but we built and operated transportation systems. Most importantly, the three thousand employees saw our new mission clearly. Soon, I had employees, consultants and even the general public coming to my office with envelopes of dollar bills saying they were collecting them from people saying, "Highway Department". Often, at functions where I would speak, the person introducing me or another speaker would say "Highway Department", then automatically pull out their wallets.

'In the beginning we used the dollars to give to charity at Thanksgiving and Christmas. Then, in August 2005, Hurricane Katrina hit the Gulf Coast. 180 employees of the Mississippi Department of Transportation lost their homes that day. We decided that we should give our dollars to our brothers and sisters of the Mississippi DOT. We added to our dollars by having fundraisers and were able to give them a check for $10,000.00!'

Self-Management of Mistakes

Of course making a mistake can make you feel bad, but most mistakes can be fixed without big consequences. So be vigilant in your work, but don't be too hard on yourself when you make a mistake. How you deal with it will reflect on your character, and it's up to you to make it into something positive.

One of my favorite bumper stickers is 'No rain, no rainbows!' If we look for life's rainbows that inevitably come after the perpetual rain, we grow to appreciate the rain more. For with the rain comes perspective, growth, and some of life's most glorious lessons. The key lies in only letting ourselves stay down for a limited time. There's nothing wrong with throwing ourselves a little self-pity party along the way, as long as we know when it's time to say goodnight to the only guest at the party – ourself. How do we move from the rain stage to the appreciation-of-the-rainbow stage?

Get away from your environment, and engage yourself in play. Do something to break the pattern of feeling sorry for yourself, and escape the vibes of a bad day. Take a walk in the park, visit a toy store at lunch and buy yourself something fun ... or you can go ahead and dye your hair, change your name, and move to another country. Really, it's all up to you.

Throw Yourself a Party from the Joy Fund

Why not surprise yourself with something special? I think all of us need a 'joy fund'. What is a joy fund, you ask? It grows by taking a little bit of your salary each month and putting it aside for times when you need a little pick-me-up. When the time comes and you've been overworked, or you feel a little down, you use that money to make yourself feel better. For instance, send yourself something that you truly like and that would achieve the purpose of making you feel better. How about chocolate or flowers? These are almost always a surefire recipe for good cheer. Include a card that honors what you like best about yourself, or just have some fun by adding a little humor.

Some sample cards might look like this:

Dear Victoria,

Thanks for always doing such a great job here! We're not really sure how we could do it all without you, and we hope we never have to find out. I know we don't always appreciate you as much as we should, but please realize that you are THE most important part of the team, and by far the most stylish, too! Truly, we are eternally grateful that you are here.

Love, Victoria

Or maybe something a little more self-indulgent and fun:

> *Dear Victoria,*
>
> *You are IT! Is it my imagination, or do you just keep getting better looking? You should be in a museum, you piece of work! I love you like no other.*
>
> *Victoria*

Or if you want to stir up the curiosity of those around you, you might want to sign it 'Your Secret Admirer'. (Warning: This is guaranteed to spark some envy and start rumors in the office.)

How Could This Be Worse?

Another way to celebrate when things go wrong is by playing the game 'How could this be worse?' By asking yourself this question, it helps you immediately put things in perspective, and then things don't really seem so bad.

Let's say, for instance, that you made a big mistake which has set you back in meeting your finish line. You feel the weight of the world on your shoulders, and you're feeling like you will never finish this project on time. Then you play the 'How could this be worse?' game.

It could be worse if ... your computer crashed and you lost all the work on the project, ouch! Or if there were a terrible fire, and not only did you lose your work, but you also lost your entire house. Double ouch! Or worst of all, your house burned down, you lost all of your work, and your daughter ran off with a clown from the circus – both of whom are now in jail accused of (add your worst nightmare in here). Okay, enough is enough – move quickly from these thoughts, and be grateful that your situation is none of the above.

Celebrating mistakes in a clever way – one that helps illustrate the lessons learned – helps build a culture of trust, acceptance, resilience and innovation.

In Summary

Successes – as well as lessons learned – are important to celebrate, as well as surprisingly easy to do so. Investing a little time will yield major dividends for you, your employees, and your company!

- Break success down into small, easily evaluated steps, and celebrate the milestones along the way.
- Catch people doing something right.
- Customize your appreciation for each employee.
- Be specific in your appreciation: What, so what, now what?
- Take the time to celebrate yourself.
- Have a personal celebration ritual.
- Learn from the mistakes made by yourself and others.
- Celebrate these mistakes and find the rainbow in the rain!

Don't be afraid to take risks when it comes to celebrating. People will appreciate your efforts, and you will gain much more than you may imagine. As investments go, a celebration is one of the most cost-efficient ways to upgrade your company. And best of all, the dividends – both material and personal – will keep accumulating for days, months, and years to come.

Chapter 4 Celebrating Community

Wherever two or more are gathered, you can call it a community. And when there's a community, there's a cause for a celebration. Our communities are a reflection of who we have become, as together people from all the groups in our lives: family, friends, and co-workers; people we commune with at the gym; the bank; the religious organization; or even those we see every day on the bus or at the cafe. And the more opportunities we have to celebrate these communities, the more enriched and fulfilled our lives will be.

BUILDING COMMUNITY

The most critical element in creating community is that of trust. In Mandarin context, the word for 'trust' is *xin*. Once you have xin, then it is implied that I will take care of you, and you will take care of me.

And how do you develop xin? You do so by having integrity, doing what you say you're going to do, promoting open, honest communication, and maintaining transparency in an organization.

Beyond trust, the element of personal responsibility is also critically important. Too often, there (and elsewhere, for that matter) we rely on others to 'get the party started'. But the truth is, happiness and celebration with your community starts with YOU. It's your responsibility to bring your 'A' game to work. And 'A', in this case, is for attitude.

It's More Than a Job – It's a Community

One of the most important and constant communities we have is the one at our workplace. Keeping your GPS mindset set to 'on' and understanding the nature of your community from the inside out will take you and your organization to new levels of health and happiness.

The following examples illustrate how communities can work together in action – as well as in fun!

It Takes a Village

We can learn a lot from Davita, the largest kidney dialysis company in the world, based in Denver, Colorado. They refer to their company as a 'village', with the CEO, Kevin Tiry, being their 'mayor.' It's a democratic society, with all employees being equal members of the village. It's 'One for all, and all for one' ... or rather, 'One for all, and all for fun'.

When you choose to become a citizen of this village, you make a decision to engage your head, your heart, and your hands for the greater good for those around you. You commit to living the values of the village. In other words, you become part of a big, wonderful extended family, connected by a common purpose: that of becoming a world-class health care organization, together.

So you may be wondering: how can I make my organization more of a village? One way is to take the advice of Ken Blanchard.

Catch People Doing Something Right

Ken Blanchard has been talking about taking care of your employees for over thirty years. In his very first book, *The One-Minute Manager*, Ken shares the importance of catching people doing something right. Managers should spend a good deal of their time wandering around, catching people doing a good job. Give your staff lots of praise along the way, and you're guaranteed to get better performance. Then, when it comes time to have the hard conversations, they'll be better received by the employees. By then they'll know that you are aware of their strengths, and that you've cared enough to notice these first.

The Company That Plays Together...

A recurring theme in this book is that of the importance of play – both in and out of the work environment. There's no question that one of the best ways to celebrate community is to play together. The following examples of workplace community play shows how 'the organization that plays together, stays together'!

SCB's Got Talent

One special celebration that engages employees and creates a lot of fun throughout the many offices of Standard Chartered Bank is 'SCB's Got Talent'. This festive event gives each employee a chance to show off their (often surprising) talents. You can imagine the excitement that erupts when the gang realizes that quiet Suzanne in the back office can belt out a soul tune to rival Beyoncé, or that timid teller Steve can make a guitar wail Van Halen-style!

Winners from each country then compete in a global competition, with those finalists getting to play the big stage at Global Leadership events for the bank.

This stellar event illustrates how far a company will go to create connection and celebration. Honoring employees' personal talents will instantly build enthusiasm, create new connections (and upgrade old ones), and create a new level of team cohesiveness.

Singing Your Praises

Want to honor and surprise your colleagues while raising money for a good cause? Let your Celebration Committee choose a few talented members to dress up in costume and become a singing telegram. Employees can pay to have kind and funny words sung to their fellow co-workers. The money then goes to a cause that is near and dear to the company.

Department of Liking Other Departments

Chester Elton from the Orange Revolution gave us a great idea about how a department can celebrate other departments. How about installing a traveling award – a symbolic object of some sort – which goes from department to department every month? Each month's winner then chooses the next month's winner. Making this choice opens up discussions about what different departments are doing well, as well as how their successes are improving the company. What a great way to get departments talking to one another. The focus stays on the positive, in keeping with the fun and the spirit of the award. A brilliant idea in celebrating community!

Whether through your own version of a popular reality show, a traveling trophy, or another celebratory event or ritual, one thing is clear: it's got to be 'all for one' – and that means everyone is included.

COMMUNITY: A TAPESTRY OF MANY THREADS

Time and again, the topic of Diversity has come up in our research. Let's face it, in an international corporate world, diversity is no longer an exception; rather, it's the rule. And having many different 'threads' in the tapestry of an organization is a great strength from a world-context standpoint. Almost everyone we've spoken with believes that inclusion of *all* employees is critical in making a community celebration successful.

Different People, Same Celebration

But what is Diversity? Even the concept itself can have diverse meanings: diversity of gender, nationality, age, belief systems, etc. To make celebrating diversity one of your organization's strengths, we have three important tips from Lenora Billings-Harris, an Inclusion/Diversity expert whom we interviewed:

1) Make sure to include everyone in the celebration. Involve as many different types of people as possible in the planning committee to ensure that everyone feels comfortable and honored. If food is served, offer a wide variety so that all people – regardless of religious or dietary restrictions – can enjoy the bounty. Help every person understand the importance of his or her role in creating a successful, celebratory event.
2) Be keenly aware of your own behavior, sense of acceptance (versus judgment), and overall worldview. Be respectful in the language you use when addressing others' differences – whether social, racial, or religious.
3) Honor diversity in your policies and procedures. An organization is less likely to encounter issues regarding diversity when diversity is clearly respected and celebrated from the top down.

Celebrating Diversity Out Loud

So how do we effectively and constructively convey our positive attitudes about diversity – both personally and as an organization?

For one thing, we cannot expect clarity – or, for that matter, respect or celebration – if we continue to tiptoe around our differences. Don't be afraid to talk openly in a Town Hall-type meeting about the issues of diversity as well as the sometimes differing needs across generations and nationalities. To help facilitate discussion, you might even show a television or movie clip which shows blatant diversity issues. Encourage open, respectful sharing sessions around the topic to further promote positive behaviors and attitudes around diversity.

Power to the (Diverse) People

Appoint ambassadors from different cultures to share brand values and varying customs with other employees. Having a range of ambassadors from diverse backgrounds in your organization will help represent the true spectrum of differences among your staff. This, in turn, helps everyone feel heard and valued. David Thomas from Standard Chartered Bank based in Hong Kong, and Jun Maria Tan Abdullah from MIMOS in Malaysia, both agree that this is a very powerful way to engage people and to honor the diversity of the culture.

Let your organization celebrate that which each individual celebrates with family. Let different nationalities help plan the celebrations close to their hearts – which will surely increase the authenticity of the celebration and allows other employees a snapshot into that particular culture.

For example, Susan Barrett told us that in her organization, National Exchange Carrier Association, the Japanese New Year is celebrated with her Japanese colleague George bringing in Japanese snacks and then telling the good fortune of each person based on the Japanese zodiac sign. Susan says it is great fun. Celebrate the diversity in your community, and you're well on your way to creating a culture of celebration.

On Culture and Rhythm: Jitske Kramer, Corporate Anthropologist, Author of *Managing Cultural Dynamics*

My friend and respected colleague Jitske Kramer has spent many years studying culture, digging deep into what elements combine to create the most successful and connected companies and communities. She has shared some of her wisdom for this book – wisdom that will surely help you in thinking about the culture of your own organization in a new light. Thank you, Jitske, for these important thoughts:

> Even amidst all the differences in experience and all the diversity that exists around the globe, there are a few key elements that connect all human beings on a deep level. One of these is the need to play, dance, and make music. Everywhere you travel, you will find people playing drums, singing, clapping and dancing. Some of us may believe that the musical instruments themselves are responsible for creating the beat. This, however, is false. The rhythms of the music come from within ourselves. How else could one explain the close relationship that manifests between music and ethnicity? It is our inner rhythm, which we amplify when we make music.

This is an important notion for those of us seeking to create a culture of celebration. When your inner compass is geared towards gratitude and appreciation, the people around you are more likely to tune into this celebratory mood. In other words: turning on your GPS (your Celebration Mindset of Gratitude, Play and Surprise) is like setting your inner tone to a positive rhythm. You are, in essence, creating a vibe with which people around you want to synchronize.

Let me spend a few words to explain the wonder and importance of the words 'rhythm' and 'synchronize' in the context of creating a culture of celebration. Rhythm, like gravity, is a hidden force binding groups together. This remarkable phenomenon heavily impacts our lives. In fact, when we are unable to synchronize with the people around us, our levels of anxiety and uncertainty rise. When, on the other hand, a group of people is in sync, they seem to move or think like one body. If one person loses the rhythm, the entire group process is disrupted. As stated by cultural anthropologist Edward Hall: 'The capacity – in fact, the drive – to stay in sync is innate, and whatever rhythms are developed by a culture will be adhered to by most members.'

When we take this knowledge and apply it towards creating a culture of celebration in our workplaces, we see the need to create a positive 'rhythm' of appreciation and gratitude – one to which people can synchronize. If we lose the 'beat' and get lost in negativity, chances are high that those around us will in turn tune into an undesirable dance.

The only way, then, to start a positive beat is by playing our own personal tune of celebration. In this way, you are literally 'setting the tone' for increased connections and synchronicity within your community.

FROM A PERFECT COMMUNITY TO A PERFECT WORLD

Creating community can extend out as far as the entire globe. Yet it may also be a small-scale operation, one that happens between and among members on a team or in an office. Once we understand how that community looks, acts, and thrives from the inside out, we'll be better equipped to take it to the next level.

Here I'd like to share a few personal experiences in the community of my own then-young organization. Yes, it's true, even back then, Scott Friedman & Associates was founded on the not-too-ambitious prospect of creating a perfect world ...

'Perfect World'

After one year of working together, I met with Nancy, my Director of Everything, to discuss how we might better serve our clients and each other. It was out of this discussion that the 'Perfect World' concept was born. How could we create each other's Perfect World? Wouldn't it be nice in our employer/employee relationship if we created a situation in which we both did more of what we loved, outsourced what we didn't like, made it a point to do everything possible to make sure the other is happy, and remained focused on living true to our best values? What a concept!

In fact, what if we all decided that an emphasis in our job descriptions would be to simply create one another's Perfect World? Simple, yet profound.

My Perfect World

'Okay,' Nancy asked, 'What is it for you? What drives you? What do you value? What is your Perfect World?'

'It's having more joy and less hassle in my life,' I said. 'It's freedom to come and go as I please, freedom to create, and freedom to make a difference in this world in the ways I'd like. If you help me do that, I'll be one happy boss.'

Nancy's Perfect World

'Okay, Nancy, your turn. What is your Perfect World?' I asked.

'For me it's getting rid of anything to do with accounting and technology, and having more time for marketing and taking care of our clients. I'd also like to spend more time with my son (who was 12 at the time) and with my family around the country. I'd like to travel more, have more fun, and partake in the delightfully unexpected more often.'

'Okay, done,' I replied. 'No more accounting and technology. We'll order out. This will free you up to do more marketing and to spend more time with clients. You can 'call in well' anytime you like if it gives you the opportunity to be with David and the family. We'll create an incentive plan, and your reward will be free tickets to travel anywhere you'd like to meet up with David. And I'll do my best to keep things from getting mundane in the workplace. Then, at the end of every month, we'll grade ourselves on a scale of 1-10 on how well we've done at creating each other's Perfect World. If we both aren't at a 9 or a 10, we'll figure out a way to raise the score the next month.'

And for the last 23 years, we've stayed in tune with each other's Perfect World and have created and expanded our professional community in the same spirit.

The Perfect Birthday Surprise!

Even more fun in creating community at our office happens when family members are invited into the pursuit of that Perfect World. As a basketball fan, I often think of this as a team sport. The court is your office, the team is your group of employees (and you), and the crowd is the community around it all. The more you can include everyone, the better the game.

This in mind, Nancy's 50th birthday was a true slam-dunk (complete with the roaring crowd!). David, her son, and her husband, Jack, joined forces with me to together etch a perfect plot.

David called about three weeks out and said, 'Mom I feel terrible, but I can't come home for your birthday. I have two tests that week, and I can't make them up. What if I come home two weeks later, and we'll have more time to spend together?' Nancy was disappointed, but she understood.

Fast forward to July 7, 1999 – Nancy's 50th birthday. Being the loyal employee she is, Nancy is working a half day. At around ten o'clock, the phone rings. It's my buddy Tim, but Nancy thinks it's a client. I answer and say, 'You've made a decision, and you'd like me to speak on October 23rd in Orlando?' (I cover the phone) ... 'Nancy, could you please do me a quick favor? Take my keys, run to the car, and get my road calendar out of the trunk. Thanks!' (She'd done this before when I'd forgotten to bring in my calendar.) She gets there, opens the trunk, and her son David jumps out and screams, 'SURPRRIIIIIIISSEEE!'

Once we revived Nancy, she knew she was somewhere in the vicinity of her Perfect World. David had been happy to play along and was certainly glad he survived his time in the trunk. It was only six hours ... just kidding!

Creating Others' Perfect Worlds

So what if we could all live our lives with each other's 'Perfect Worlds' in mind? What if we spent more time asking questions and paying attention to the Perfect World wishes of our co-workers, employees, customers, spouses, family, friends, tribes, and outer communities? What if we made choices in life based upon these perfect worlds? Would we sell more?

Would we laugh more? Would we love more? Would the quality of our relationships improve? Would the quality of our lives improve? Can you imagine how much more we'd all have to celebrate?

Perfection May Be Closer Than You Think

So how can one best go about creating another person's 'Perfect World'? You start by looking at the world through their eyes. It's not always easy if you only have eyes for 'I'. Get past your self-absorbed self. The world does not revolve around you, though when caught in the 'I', it may appear so. Pay more attention, and realize that everyone else has an 'I' too. If you practice breaking out of that tunnel vision, you'll be better able to create that Perfect World with more authenticity and connection.

Start by asking questions. For instance, you can ask the customers directly: 'If we could have done one thing better in working with you, what would it have been?' Find out, and then be willing to deliver. You can also ask yourself: *How can I create a better experience for my customers? What can I do to truly connect with them? How can I move from being ordinary to being extraordinary?*

Think of it this way: Do you want to keep good employees? How about good customers? Or, for that matter, good friends? If so (and I think you do), find out what motivates them – what they live for. Find out about their Perfect World. Ask questions with an open mind and a willing intention.

Remember, the Perfect World concept causes a natural ripple effect. For each person whose life you improve, he or she will become more likely to do the same for others. Therefore, one Perfect World just might lead to another and then another ... resulting a more perfect world for us all.

Call me ambitious ...

In Summary

- Look for opportunities to celebrate all of your communities.
- Catch people doing something right.
- Make sure everyone feels included in community celebrations.
- Be aware of your own behavior, sense of acceptance, and overall worldview.
- Honor diversity in your dai y life, as well as in your policies and procedures.
- Seek to create a 'Perfect World' for others – from those closest to you presently to those who may benefit down the road.

You're on a mission – an important one we share – and my hope it that you will choose to accept it. If you really want to create an authentic community, make sure that every member is a part, each working towards his or her highest purpose with a sense of celebration.

As Ralph Waldo Emerson once said: 'One of the most beautiful compensations of this life is that no one can sincerely try to help another without helping himself.' To me this speaks of an ideal foundation for true community, one Perfect World at a time. What a wonderful way to live!

Chapter 5 Celebrating Well-Being

These days, employee well-being is far too important a matter to overlook if you're out to stay competitive. It's no longer just a luxury that the best and most admired companies can afford to address. Instead, it's an element you can no longer afford to overlook. In today's competitive market, a company that listens and cares is what the top of the employee pool seeks and expects, and rightly so.

With your GPS turned on and tuned in, you'll find it easy to put your attention towards your most important assets of all: those who spend their days making your company tick. Soon enough, you'll come to see that celebrating the well-being of your employees is a win-win endeavor, as doing so will reap far-reaching rewards for everyone involved.

WELL WORTH THE EFFORTS

To get you started, let's look at current research, methods, and possibilities, as well as at companies who are already putting the 'wellness philosophy' into practice.

How May We Help You?

At Pepsico, taking care of their employees' well-being is not just lip service. Managers at the company are required to ask their employees, 'What is the one thing I can do as your manager to help create your work/life balance?'

When it's time for the manager's performance review, he or she is evaluated in part on effectiveness in assisting employees with that 'life balance' question. Each manager is also expected to serve as a life balance role model in general. This practice shows how Pepsi successfully creates a culture of encouraging and celebrating employee well-being.

Just Say Yes!

Many companies have a flexibility program, but the question is, does it truly serve the individual? Why waste company time and money on a program that may fall short in addressing the needs of your employees? You need a system that's easy and effective – one that makes a difference in employees' lives, which will ultimately make a difference in the big picture for your company.

This requires the vision and willingness to look beyond policy to clearly assess individual needs. How can you help to create your employees' perfect world? If you care enough to do this (and if you're reading this book, it's likely that you do), you'll have the right answers to questions such as these: 'Do you want to coach your son's soccer team?' And your answer? No problem!

'Do you need to work a four-day week to plan your daughter's wedding?' We can do that! 'Do you need to come in early, and then take 90 minutes at lunch to eat and work out?' We'll make it happen.

This is the sort of attitude organizations need today. Each manager should ideally be willing and able to meet these different needs. Each market has its own nuances, and managers need to be sensitive to this. Understanding the needs of employees (and striving to keep these needs met) will not only impact employee engagement, it will also attract the best employees to want to work for you.

Ultimately, your efforts in this area will become a competitive advantage. As in Pepsi's case, emphasizing well-being correlates perfectly with their brand image of being 'fun, youthful, and full of life.' It's nice to see a company that walks its talk.

Well-Being Works

Tom Rath and James Harter, co-authors of *Well-Being: The Five Essential Elements*, also make a strong case for the necessity of managers to pay attention to the well-being of their employees. In the section of the book entitled 'Career Well-Being', the authors claim that career well-being is perhaps the most important, as it touches every other area of our lives.

As the foremost voice in research-based performance management, Gallup's studies are worth noting. Gallup's research supports the idea that a leader who cares for his or her employees' well-being achieves better results. In fact, the employees of such managers tend to share the following qualities:

- A tendency to produce higher-quality work
- Less frequent illness
- Stronger loyalty to their job
- Lower likelihood of becoming injured on the job

The most caring and progressive leaders know that they are in the business of boosting their employees' well-being, and they use this knowledge as a competitive advantage to recruit and retain employees. When better relationships, financial security, vibrant physical health and productive involvement in the community are norms among a company's staff, that company will find it much easier to attract top talent. And top talent is what takes an organization to the top!

Designing Wellness

Many excellent companies have created customized wellness programs and opportunities for their employees. These programs have improved not only the individuals enjoying them, but also the organizations themselves. Below are a few that stood out in our research:

Doing Well, Being Well

One of the most forward-thinking companies in this realm is Lane Crawford Joyce Group of Hong Kong. For starters, this company has designed its office spaces with ergonomics as a priority. They check individual work stations and make recommendations for chairs, risers, keyboards, lighting, etc. which best complement their employees' physical health and well-being. Other features in their office spaces include natural light, centralized printers and storage, filtered water, communal dining areas, ping-pong tables, numerous break-out areas, Wi-Fi, a nursing room, a dedicated nap/chill area, and even a walking meditation area.

Programmed for Health

We talked to the Vice President of Group Organizational Wellness, Martha Collard, about what she is doing to promote employee well-being. Her role encompasses four high-end retailing companies with a total of staff of four thousand, mainly in Hong Kong and Greater China. One thousand staff members in total are housed in their new corporate offices in Aberdeen.

Martha's well-being assistant, Alex, has a fixed schedule wherein he spends two afternoons a week in the stores giving shoulder and neck massages, along with short workshops on Theraband stretching and 'deskercise' (exercises/stretches you can do at your desk). What a great way to bring energy to the work day! As you may imagine, this program is very popular, and soon the warehouse staff will benefit, too.

Other health and well-being benefits offered at the company include: body massages in the office twice a week (offered by retrained workers from the YWCA), personal onsite consultations by qualified healers, exercise ball classes at lunchtime, community yoga classes in the evening, and a recently established Employee Assistance Program.

But wait, there's more! To keep the spirit of play alive at 3 p.m. on most days, Alex rotates through each department with iPod and speakers in hand to do five minutes of 'I Like to Move it', King Julian's theme song in Madagascar. He also leads staff members in other fun activities, including balloon volleyball, relay races, the Macarena – anything to get them up and out of their seats, moving and laughing and energized for the rest of the afternoon.

For those interested in more strenuous exercise, Martha has founded what she calls her '"A" Team' of young, fit men and women interested in keeping in top physical shape. So far they have started a jogging club (some completed a recent marathon), friendly soccer matches, and (in warmer weather) badminton, dragon boating, and swimming. Martha continually surveys the company to see what other groups might be started, based on the mutual interests of the employees. (Beekeeping and organic gardening have already been proposed for the rooftop!)

Aside from the physical well-being of the staff, Martha also focuses on the spiritual and emotional components through a two-day program called 'Me, Myself, and You'. To date, she has worked with nearly three hundred members of the management team to 'know thyself' through psychometrics. Her weekly 'Martha Messages' feature themes such as rekindling the spirit at work, identifying your passion at work, and living your values.

Through them she helps guide staff in passing on a 'whole person' philosophy of well-being.

A Bull's-Eye for Wellness

The SCOOTER Store is another company that celebrates healthy living with their employees. In 2008 they kicked off a targeted wellness endeavor, branded 'Live. Work. Be. Well'. They began with a no-fee onsite fitness center, along with a free-for-employees medical clinic (also onsite) operated by a third party.

Their monthly wellness themes are reinforced through newsletter articles and bulletin boards. They also encourage participation in annual exercise events, such as their own Couch Potato 5K Run/Walk for employees and their families, as well as the MS (Multiple Sclerosis) 150 Bike Race and the American Heart Association Heart Walk.

In addition, they offer free biometric screenings to all employees every year. Biometric Testing provides an immediate assessment of a member's basic health and wellness indicators, including:

- Blood Pressure (High, Low and/or Normal)
- Cholesterol/Lipids (HDL and LDL)
- Body Mass Index (BMI)
- Blood Glucose/Blood Sugar

Clearly, the SCOOTER Store has its customers' best health in mind, which is why the company is in excellent health as well!

Eat, Drink, and Be Healthy

A well-rounded (pun intended) wellness program will also address the importance of a healthy diet. That's because eating well is beneficial – for both the waistline and the bottom line.

You can help your employees become more mindful of healthy eating in a number of ways. For instance, you can offer delicious, wholesome foods in the employee cafeteria. Better yet, have salads, fruits, and other healthy items available in the snack room at all times. You might even name a special 'health snack' day – such as 'Fruity Fridays' – when the specialty foods (in this case, fruits) are available in beautiful, healthful arrangements in the break room. And why not host a potluck with a health food theme, then ask each employee to bring in something yummy to eat that supports the theme (and their best habits!)? Eating for health becomes easier when you make a celebration of it with your colleagues. Sharing a nutritious, delicious diet with colleagues helps motivate the group habit towards healthy choices while building a healthy (literally!) team spirit.

Need more of an emphasis on weight loss as well? Encouraging participation in public sports events for charity will provide a springboard for colleagues to get together in the name of health. There are even specific events aimed at promoting weight loss in a team setting. One such event is the Lose2Win Challenge, a contest wherein individuals or teams compete to lose weight and reduce body fat percentage.

MINDING OUR OWN WELLNESS – AS WELL AS THAT OF EMPLOYEES

Research shows that a healthy state of mind – which includes a strong sense of purpose along with balance and a sense of joy – is critical to our overall well-being. Companies that address well-being as a priority understand this, as the examples below illustrate.

From Strength to ... Satisfaction

According to *Well Being* and Gallup's research, one of the essentials of enjoyment at work is having the opportunity to use one's strengths every day. Employees who do use their strengths are six times as likely to report having an excellent quality of life: 'People who use their strengths every day can enjoy a full 40-hour work week, while those who do not get burned out after just 20 hours of work per week.' (Rath and Harter)

Google is one company doing a banner job of encouraging employees to work to their strengths. In fact, they allow their engineers to spend 20 per cent of their time working on something they find fun – something that stirs their passion. Not surprisingly, it has been during this 20 per cent 'free' time that some of their most ground-breaking products and services were initially developed – innovations such as iGoogle, Google Maps, Personalized Search, Google Docs, Google Reader, Google Groups, Google Goggles, and Google Moderator.

This shows how creation happens best when we feel free and 'in our element'... an important lesson to learn if you are seeking well-being, both in and out of your organization.

Care for a Cigar With That Movie?

I conducted an interview with Mike Abrashoff, Captain of *USS Benfold*. This 'GPS-attuned' captain turned the worst-performing ship in the US Navy into the best – by listening to his staff and then by acting on what he heard. Mike asked himself, *How would I want my family to be treated if they were part of this organization?* and then treated them in that spirit. He helped enhance his staff's well-being by empowering them to take ownership of the ship and make their own decisions.

He asked the crew, 'How can we have fun on this ship?' and followed up on many of the ideas. He says, 'Once your people know you care, celebration becomes easy.'

Mike shared a funny anecdote about the importance of celebration in relieving stress in a difficult, pressure-filled work environment:

At night, most Navy ships turn off their lights in order to remain unseen by hostile ships. So, to enjoy a relaxing evening, he set up a projector and used the sail of his ship to show a movie to the staff while enjoying freshly-popped popcorn. This inventive way of de-stressing led another US Navy ship to come by and enjoy the movie too! And Friday night was 'Jazz and Cigar Night' on the back deck.

Freedom of Movement, Freedom of Mind

Microsoft is one organization doing an excellent job in sustaining that healthy work/life balance for their employees. As a rule, they allow their employees to work from home whenever they feel the need to do so. This helps alleviate the pressure for families with newborns, those who have illness in the family, or those who require time to tend to other family responsibilities. Even their work spaces are designed to promote flexibility.

While in Amsterdam, I had the opportunity to stop by the Microsoft office. What a unique and comfortable space! It feels and looks more like a living room than it does an office. The physical divisions and departments have been replaced with an open, cooperative environment. People can work wherever they want to in the space – whether in the quiet corner between the pantry and the CEO's office, or on one of the many comfortable sofas. As long as they perform appropriately, employees and their teams can work flexibly – which goes a long way in promoting work/life balance. Healthy snacks can be found in various places, and provide needed energy for a high performance day.

All in the Family

Another trend mentioned by Tom Rath in *Well-Being* and verified in our own research is a shifting focus towards the 'whole person' approach to managing people. More care and attention is being given to employee's families, which in turn affects a staff's well-being and that work/life balance.

PepsiCo's Family-Friendly Policies

One way that Pepsi celebrates family well-being is by having a 'flex finish time', which allows employees to come in early and leave early. In addition, the company respects weekend time by making it a point to avoid late meetings on Fridays. Weekend travel for work is always compensated with a refund in time or days. The company discourages emailing on the weekends for work. If you do, don't expect a response from your colleagues until Monday. They're all out celebrating and recharging – at least that's the hope and the goal!

Ladies' Clubs

Essar Steel of India also knows the importance of taking care of the family. The company has created Ladies' Clubs in each of their offices. These clubs celebrate family life with many diverse community programs, from cooking demonstrations to Independence Day celebrations to philanthropic activities to help those in need.

Thoughtful Family Gestures

Some companies will send cards, flowers, or useful gifts to an employee's family members just to thank them for their support as well as for the key role they play in promoting the employee's well-being. We heard many examples of creative ways companies have shown their gratitude to families. This is a wonderful, inexpensive way to improve the company's brand image while engaging employees and their families along the way.

The bottom line is this: Pay attention to the things your employee shares about his or her family. You may find the perfect clay frog to add to a son's toy amphibian collection or that special doll another's daughter has been seeking. A simple thoughtful gesture will not soon be forgotten.

And the Prize Goes to ... Good Health!

How about rewarding your employees' efforts at healthy behavior? Why not give prizes for those who avoid taking sick leave, or create a point system for healthy living outside the workplace?

In the book *1001 Ways to Reward Employees*, Bob Nelson describes how Pioneer Natural Resources Company offers a $700 bonus to employees who do (and don't do) the following: they exercise three times a week, they don't smoke, they don't take sick days, and they don't submit major medical claims. Thanks to this incentive, the company health care costs have been reduced to 25 per cent below the industry average. The connection is clear, and the result is exactly what we all seek, isn't it?

A Few More Ways

Bob Nelson shares two more excellent examples of how companies take care of employees from a family/well-being standpoint.

One of these is JP Morgan Chase & Company. They offer back-up childcare for employees who need it. This has saved the company an estimated $820,000 as a result of lower absenteeism.

Wilton Connor Packaging is happy to lighten the load of household tasks for their employees. How? Employees simply bring their laundry to work. The company then sends it off to be washed, dried and folded.

'Honey, look what I got done at work today!'

Need more ideas on how to celebrate employee well-being? Here are just a few:

- Family off hours
- Family Day four times per year
- Bring Your Children (or Pet) to Work Day
- Adding spouse's and children's birthdays to your managers' calendars for acknowledgement
- Celebrating the academic (or other) achievements of your employees' children
- Daddy Day (where fathers are encouraged to take a day off to visit their children's school/sporting events/etc.)

In Summary

One of the most important ongoing celebrations at work is that of taking care of your employees' well-being on a day-to-day basis. Honoring families and finding ways to improve each individual's work/life balance is an important – and ultimately a profitable – policy to adopt.

- Start by asking, 'What is one thing I, as your manager, can do to help create your work/life balance?'
- Tailor individual needs to your well-being policy.
- Give people a chance to utilize their strengths every day, and their well-being will improve.
- Reward (and encourage) positive, healthy behavior.
- Contribute to your employees' well-being by providing them with information about physical exercise, healthy eating, stress reduction, work/life balance, and mindful, healthy living.
- Involve teams in healthy eating, as well as exercise, group sporting events, and other healthful events in the office.
- Create a company culture wherein employees' families are considered an important element in the balance equation. Celebrate them as well, and watch the support system around your organization grow and thrive.

Finally, as you're nurturing the work/life balance among your employees, don't forget to model the same in your own life. As Ingvar Kamprad, founder of IKEA puts it, 'If there is such a thing as good leadership, it is to give a good example.'

In this case, a 'good example' means keeping on your own GPS, taking excellent care of your health – including eating well, controlling stress, and exercising – and maintaining that work/ family balance you are seeking for your staff members.

Once your employees see that you are well and balanced, taking the next steps to follow suit will be much easier. And, from this shared fertile ground of well-being, your company will grow and flourish. Now's that's something to celebrate!

Chapter 6 Celebrating With Compassion

My favorite part of conducting our interviews was listening to stories from companies who are doing good things to serve their communities. Reaching out to help others as an organization is more than just the 'right thing to do'. It can bring teams and organizations together in meaningful ways, attract attention to causes (not to mention to the company, and for all the right reasons), and increase a company's effectiveness even beyond its business pursuits.

Perhaps most importantly, becoming involved in community service sets a precedent for others to follow suit. It is part of the recipe for true leadership – which makes excellent business sense, doesn't it?

WANTED: A COMPANY THAT CARES

According to research by psychologist and emotional health expert Dr Steven Stein of Multi-Health, the number one predictor of employee retention is the emotional intelligence attribute of social responsibility. Employees are loyal to companies that are doing good things in the world.

Our research revealed that employees of today show strong preferences about what an ideal work situation looks like. Time and again, we heard from people who want to work with a company that has these qualities:

- Is socially responsible
- Seeks and maintains involvement in good causes (employees want to take pride in what their organizations stand for)
- Takes care of their employees in good and bad times Compassion programs score high marks for attraction and retention. We heard many wonderful examples of organizational programs specifically set up to take care of employees who had fallen on hard times.

Organized for Good

Many organizations are fulfilling this 'wish list' for prospective and current employees – as well as for the community. These companies illustrate how coming together for a cause can have maximum impact and lasting positive effects. Here are just a few examples of the many efforts at helping the community, shared by organizations in our research:

And Speaking of Giving...

The National Speakers Association (NSA), of which I am a proud member and past President, has its own fund: the Professional Speaker Benefit Fund (PSBF). We raise money through several channels, including through members, educational events, social events, and lots of other creative pursuits. We've raised a few million dollars and, whenever personal tragedy strikes, the NSA Foundation's PSBF fund is there to help ease the pain by giving up to $10,000. It's a wonderful benefit of membership, knowing that your association is looking out for you when things get tough.

Building Homes, Strengthening Teams

A few years back, I worked with the leadership team of Alcatel-Lucent in Cambodia. One entire day was devoted to building houses for the underprivileged out in the countryside of Phnom Penh. After a day of labor with over a hundred leaders of the Asia Pacific team, we watched as the families moved into houses we had just helped to build. The families were so grateful to have an upgrade in living conditions, and I trust that the Alcatel-Lucent team was profoundly moved by this gratitude – as well as by the opportunity to make a difference. I know I was. From that day forward, I created my team-building programs around the shared vision of helping a cause of some kind.

One Week to Do Good

The company Netapp, which consistently appears on various 'best employers in the world' lists, allows their employees to take a week off (paid) to do any volunteer work they want. According to Dorsey Delavigne, an engineer we interviewed, the volunteer work can involve anything from working in a youth home to traveling to Africa to helping build a school. Of all the companies we've interviewed, no other company has more fully or generously facilitated the efforts of employees to actively support a good cause.

Cycling for CSR

Every Wednesday, The SCOOTER Store sends four volunteers to help deliver meals to senior citizens in New Braunfels. The company has been doing this for ten years, and every year the number of volunteers grows. The volunteers pick up a number of prepared meals and take them to homes all over town. Many of the seniors receiving them may not otherwise eat due to illness, lack of mobility, etc. Thanks to the SCOOTER Store and these volunteers, their quality of life is improved. And, for their efforts, the volunteers involved are celebrated at an annual luncheon.

The SCOOTER store's community efforts don't stop there. Every year, they host a Valentine's Day balloon sale at the store to benefit the Children's Advocacy Center. They supply the balloons and helium. Volunteers from the center blow up the balloons and sell them to employees. The most recent event raised more than $4000 for the center. Employees buy them for their managers and co-workers, and the balloons stay floating for at least a couple of weeks.

Tata Group

The Tata group from India is globally known – not only for their wide range of quality products, but also for their contributions to charity. In fact, a large part of the Tata Group's profits are returned to the Trusts (charities) that are also the main shareholders of the group's holding company, Tata Sons.

We interviewed Amar Sinhji, Head of Human Resources at Tata Capital, asking him how the company shows compassion to their employees and the community. Amar told us that Tata contributes to many non-governmental organizations and charities as well as to a number of the many religious and cultural celebrations in India. It is a basic premise of every Tata company to give back to their own communities through service and/or support. Every Tata company has a very detailed corporate sustainability plan and strategy.

In the case of natural disasters, most Tata Group employees voluntarily give a full day's salary (or more) to the families or communities who have been affected. The parent company will often match the total amount collected from these generous employees with an equal contribution. For larger disasters, such as the 2011 tsunami in Japan or other natural disasters around the world, the Tata group sends support to the site – both financially and in active support. Volunteers have been known to stay for days or weeks to help rebuild the community.

When faced with the untimely death of a member of the Tata family, the company has often pitched in, not only with short-term financial support, but also with an employment offering to another family member – thereby helping the deceased employee's family secure a financially stable future after the tragedy.

Ways to Raise Funds: Endless Possibilities

There are more possible ways to raise funds than there are words in this book. Use your imagination, and make it happen. You can be creative, even combining the service with your own company's business and/or training objectives.

Here's one example of a lighthearted way to reinforce important messages while raising money for a good cause: a company scavenger hunt. In the hunt, you send your employees to places that have significance to their learning. Once they take find a clue and/or take a photo at that location, they proceed to the next place. For every place visited and photo taken, a set amount of money is given to a cause chosen by a staff vote. For example, let's say you want your staff to know more about the competition. Your five places on the scavenger hunt might include your competition's stores, where they go to learn specific things about specific products. The team that comes back first wins a prize, and the company also makes a donation to the selected cause. Thanks, Brenda Bence, for this great idea!

This is just one of the myriad possibilities for fundraising. Remember, too, that any amount will help your cause. It's as much about the journey – the team-building, the learning, the increased awareness, and all the other good that comes from reaching out in the community – as it is about the money.

The Good Business of Caring for the Environment

Every organization in our time should strongly consider taking an active approach to caring for the environment. Even the small daily choices a company makes reflect its attitudes about either caring for, or being careless of, the Earth's health. If you haven't already, consider making changes to move your company forward in this realm.

Here are a few ideas: Start a recycling program (these days it's fairly simple), purchase only biodegradable and recyclable paper for offices, choose earth-friendly partyware for events and picnics, conserve water, install solar panels, use lower-energy bulbs in the office. If we all make a commitment to 'go green' together, we can continue to make an impact and help save our planet.

'Walking Your Talk' and Making a Difference

What you do as an individual reflects upon your organization, and vice versa. Therefore, making giving a part of your own life will spill over in helping you lead your organization towards doing the same. Below are a few examples of what it looks like on some of the 'front lines' in making a difference.

FROM HOMELESSNESS TO HOPEFULNESS

During our research, we had the honor of chatting with Erik Lehmann from the Dream Catalyst. He helps kids facing challenges such as poverty and homelessness live their dreams. As a man who was himself homeless as child, Erik is a mentor who personally understands their situation. He helps these kids feel special and guides them towards hope and action. Through his efforts, children feel empowered and inspired to improve the future for themselves and create a better life. Kudos to Erik – love the cause!

Erik is now working on a project called 'Homeless to Honolulu'. His vision is to inspire at least ten kids who are or were challenged by homelessness to join him in running the Honolulu Marathon this December. The accomplishment these children will celebrate from crossing that finish line – and the symbolic power they will realize – is truly limitless!

Recently, Erik worked with a student who is currently homeless apart from his college dorm room. Erik coached him and advocated with him on his campus, and now this amazing student is launching a Dream Catalyst chapter on his own campus!

I asked Erik how he celebrates, and I admired his response. He said, 'In watching these kids smile and enjoy life, I sit back, smile, and cry. That's my biggest joy.' Wow – tears of joy! Now that's a beautiful reward for a beautiful project. You, too, can help

Erik on his fantastic journey if you'd like. Take a look at www.dream-catalyst.org for more information and for ways to help. Thanks, Erik!

Helping Far and Near

I've been lucky enough to have many opportunities to enter those 'front lines' of giving – both during my years of travels and while at home in Colorado. Below I've listed a few that come to mind that may inspire you to try something new yourself. When you do, let me know. Part of what makes compassion, giving, and community service so much fun is the fact that we share it and become inspired by one another's efforts. I know that I hope to spend a lifetime finding more ways to make a difference!

Together We Can Change the World (www.twcctw.org)

I feel blessed to have a life filled with many treasured yearly rituals. One of my favorites is the 'Together We Can Change the World' tour, when we visit orphanages in Southeast Asia to raise awareness and money for homes in Cambodia, Malaysia, Thailand, Indonesia and Vietnam. We visit the children, help with household projects, and share singing and dancing, gifts, food and a a big ol' fashioned dose of love. Our goal is to help create sustainability in the orphanages, as well as to ensure that the kids get a good education. We do what we can to assist the children in becoming competent, caring, confident members of society. I always come home feeling energized and grateful. And each trip brings new friendships, tears of joy, and unforgettable memories.

Surprise ... I'm Forty!

This example requires the telling of a little story, the point of which is this: sometimes a small decision – one that costs you nothing – can offer a wonderful (and in this case, surprising!) way to make a difference for others.

It was my fortieth birthday, a milestone birthday indeed. So why not share it with friends from as many areas of my life as possible? Well, one of my 'extended families' – a group I'd known for fifteen years by this time – was a Group Home housing eight residents, each with a disability of some sort.

Once a month for those fifteen years, we'd celebrated in a variety of ways, including barbecues, croquet tournaments, birthday and holiday parties, July Fourth fireworks, sporting events, and more.

We had grown close, and as is often the case with any good friends, the residents of the home had been targets of my good-natured kidding and practical jokes. For my fortieth birthday, I thought it would be fun if they had a chance to get back at me for all that good teasing over the years. So, knowing the power of surprise, I thought that maybe they'd have a lot of fun 'surprising' me. Well, one of my friends called them and asked if they'd like to be involved in a little surprise for Scott. Of course they couldn't wait!

The day of the party came, and as the story is told from inside the house, there was plenty of excitement as they prepared for my arrival. I rang the doorbell, Bob invited me in, and there were all my Group Home buddies screaming 'Surprise!' The funny thing is, I really was surprised – surprised at how much this gesture meant to them, surprised even more at how much it meant to me. And now, eleven years later, the residents still love telling the story of the day they 'got me'.

Through working with the Group Home residents, I've learned a great deal about compassion. Although some of these friends have mental or other developmental challenges, they are never short on showing or enjoying the true spirit of friendship. As Cavett Robert said, 'No one cares how much you know until they know how much you care.' And, in this case, the caring is a two-way street.

Yes, 'got me' they did, and continue to do.

Giving Rituals: Small Gestures of Great Compassion

In the realm of giving, there are sweeping gestures that can affect tens or hundreds or even thousands of others ... but there are also small gestures that can make a person's day – and thus life – brighter. I like to call those gestures we create and repeat our 'giving rituals'.

This brand of compassion may be as simple as making it a habit to brighten the day of everyone you meet with a smile and a kind word, no matter how down you feel. It may be a ritual involving a talent you have – such as was the case with a friend of mine who made the best coffee-covered peanuts you've ever tasted. She loved celebrating her friends and clients, giving them a little treat with pick-me-up notes such as, 'I'm nuts with gratitude for you.'

There are so many ways to live a life of compassion – to 'walk your talk' and set an example for others. Even little gifts and gestures, when given wholeheartedly – compassionately – help to serve and better the world, one smile at a time. Here are a few examples of giving on the lighter side:

A Gift, Just Because

Whenever my friend Debbie Taylor travels, she brings along a gift meant for someone she's never met before. The nicely-wrapped gift is a memento from Colorado, her home state – usually either a photo book with beautiful pictures of the Colorado Rocky Mountains, or a box of famous Rocky Mountain toffee. At some point during her trip, she'll inevitably experience a special connection with someone. She'll present the gift to this person and explain her celebration ritual. It's always touching for the both the new friend and for Debbie.

Celebrating Life, $2 at a Time

One of my favorite giving rituals involves a crisp, uncirculated US $2 bill. You don't see many of these outside America. Heck, you don't see many inside America, either. I order five hundred at a time from my bank and then look for good opportunities to give them away.

Surprise! When I spend the night as a guest in someone's home or am invited for dinner, I will often hide $2 bills in unexpected places. I will open up the freezer and hide a bill in a box of frozen peas, under an ice cream container, in kitchen appliances, in cupboards, on shelves, under plants, in office equipment, inside tissue boxes, between pages in a photo album, in the cat food. No place is safe from a $2 bill when I'm around. I get calls many years later from friends telling me that they found my $2 bill under a plant that hadn't been moved for a decade.

While traveling, too, I frequently celebrate good customer service with $2 bills. From the lady at the counter to the bellman, from the busboy to the waiter to the cleaner at the airport – just about anyone might become the next $2 bill 'victim.'

Some of my favorite '$2 moments' occur in situations where tips are not normally allowed or accepted, such as at an airline ticket counter. When I get really good service from a counter ticket agent, I'll slip a $2 bill under the computer terminal when they are not looking. The agent may catch me and say, 'Mr Friedman, I'm sorry, but we cannot take tips here at United Airlines.' And I'll say, 'Ma'am, it's for good luck, and not to worry, it's *not real.*' As she holds up the bill to check for its authenticity, I'll already be headed towards the concourse. She'll more than likely find out eventually that it is real – well, that is, if she doesn't throw it away first. I know that on any given day I can look forward to putting a smile on the face of a $2 recipient ... and that opportunity in turn puts a smile on mine.

These are just a few examples – but if you look around you, you'll see many more. Start small if that feels most comfortable, then expand your circle of giving outwards, and bring everyone you can along for the wonderful ride!

In Summary

- Today's most desirable employees are seeking companies who are socially responsible (i.e. who actively support good causes) and who take care of their employees.
- Look for opportunities to do something good, and follow through with your best efforts.
- Even if you have limited financial means, there's always a way to help through your actions. Get out and get involved!
- Create your own Giving Ritual: Make giving an ongoing 'habit' or tradition in your life.
- Even small gestures of compassion can have a big and lasting impact.

Whether it's getting involved in your organization's cause or coming up with your own, maintaining a sense of compassion – and actively pursuing it through service and giving – enriches your life. The Dalai Lama put it this way: 'If you want others to be happy, practice compassion. If YOU want to be happy, practice compassion.'

I'd say the same goes for our businesses and communities too. Sounds to me like Compassion is a surefire way to a more fulfilled life of meaning and Celebration!

Chapter 7 Implementation

Congratulations! You've made it to the final chapter. That in itself is cause for celebration. Fantastico! Bravo! Yippee!

So what have you learned? Do you wake up ready to celebrate the day? Do you turn on your GPS – not the one in your car, but the one in your head and heart – the one that brings gratitude, the spirit of play, and surprise to each moment of your life? If so, and if I did my job, you're convinced of the value of celebration in most everything you do, and you're ready to make it happen. You've also seen the power of appreciation, and you've made the commitment to make gratitude an ongoing state of mind.

Do you recall the celebration scale from the first chapter? Let's return to it now that you've read the book. Okay... once again, on a scale of 1-10, what's your celebration number – and how do you get there? My hope is that you are now better able to acknowledge all the good that is happening in your life, even through the most challenging of times.

Test it and see – whatever you're doing today, whatever is in your life right now, pick something and notice how lucky you are to have or experience this. Feel yourself growing in gratitude. You've just experienced a 'mini-celebration'. Now make it a bigger one if the mood calls!

Through this book we also looked at ways to bring less hassle and more joy into each and every day. Remember, living life through celebration is a choice each of us can make. We can consciously *choose* to enjoy the journey and to treat life as our own wonder-filled, fascinating laboratory. We can choose to be excited and challenge ourselves to learn new things, which we can then celebrate, too.

GPS: A WAY OF LIFE

As we've discussed, whatever life deals us offers an opportunity to learn the lesson 'du jour.' Our mistakes, setbacks, and even tragedies offer seeds of hope, inspiration, and/or wisdom for better choices tomorrow. Turning on your GPS is the fastest way to change the reactive stress pattern we often fall prey to.

It goes like this: When you feel stressed, practice gratitude; when you feel fear, practice gratitude; when you feel anger, practice gratitude.

For true gratitude can only come from a place of humility, authenticity, and integrity. That's why when you practice being thankful, you attract more of that which you appreciate into your life. Anthony Robbins put it this way: 'When you are grateful, fear disappears and abundance appears.' **And that's when life truly will be a celebration.**

A New Day, a New Way to Celebrate

To help promote a permanent GPS mindset, ask yourself three questions every morning:

Question 1) ***What do I have to be grateful for?*** A quick reminder and appreciation of life's many blessings will wash away doubts and negativity, setting the tone for a more positive day.

Question 2) ***What do I choose to celebrate today?*** Every day, choose at least one thing for which you're grateful and for which you can plan to celebrate. Then have fun celebrating in whatever unique ways you choose. Let this gratitude and warm feeling of appreciation spill over into every other area of your life.

Question 3) ***How can I make a difference in someone's life today?*** Every day, practice at least one random act of kindness. Either choose someone to be your 'victim' of kindness first thing in the morning, or be spontaneous when the opportunity arises during the day. Either way, you'll find that there's no better feeling than making somebody else feel good.

This three-question ritual will positively change the way you look at the world and will bring more joy, abundance, and love into your life – guaranteed!

Then hop in the shower with a song in your heart, and keep the attitude of gratitude as you skip off to work, where the celebration continues. Okay, I know it may seem impossible at first, but hey – with a GPS attitude, everything is possible!

And Don't Let it Stop There...

Keep the spirit going as you continue through your day. Just flip back through this book and choose one idea on celebration to manifest. And then pick another and another.

Remember to incorporate ongoing 'micro' celebrations into your daily routine – such as picking a daily celebration word or your own theme song – to help keep you in that spirit of play, wonder, and yes, celebration.

At work, strive to break down all of your tasks and projects into incremental steps, and celebrate the milestones along the way. Don't miss celebrating a finish line!

Once you start putting into practice these and other tips shared throughout this book, you'll start enjoying work more, too. And, knowing how contagious joy can be, everyone around you will sense a difference in the energy around them ... and before long, the whole office will be breaking out in spontaneous joy and celebration.

See what you did?

IT'S UP TO YOU. YES, YOU.

It's not up to the boss, the team manager, or the doorman to get the spirit of celebration started. The only one responsible for turning an ordinary moment into one worth celebrating is YOU!

After all, now that you've read *Celebrate!* you are the official (or unofficial) Celebration Expert in your organization, as well as (even more importantly) in your life! So please, feel free to start a Celebration Revolution!

Getting Others Involved

If you can slip a copy of this book into your boss's 'must read' pile, or otherwise get your organization's leaders and HR department on board with the concept, you'll be even closer to manifesting that celebration mindset in and throughout your organization. But even if you can't get everyone behind you, you can still (and always) focus on creating little celebrations in your workplace. Then, little by little, the GPS celebration mentality will spread.

As our research points out, the more champions of celebration you have from different departments, the better. Most organizations who have successfully created a culture of celebration have a designated 'celebration team' in place. Take, for example, Intel India, winner of the third-best place to work in India in 2011, where the SPARSH team ensures that there is always something to celebrate. Employees look forward to dance competitions, parties, quarterlies, team lunches, design days, jamborees, social initiatives, I2R (Ideas to Reality), and other celebrations aimed at creating a healthy work/life balance and a strong connection between employees and leadership.

So start thinking this way: What do you have to look forward to in your organization? And what more can you CREATE to look forward to? Keep your GPS turned on, and you'll keep finding new opportunities to make every day a celebration.

Just imagine what will happen in your business when employees become truly excited just to come to work each day? When they never know what special surprise might await them, or what celebration may pop out of the corner office? How about when they look forward to the upcoming yearly review like they do to a New Year's celebration?

Winning Ingredients in a Celebration

Remember to be **culturally sensitive** and **inclusive** in your celebrations. Take into account gender, age, religious beliefs and cultural backgrounds. It is very hard to please everybody, but if you do your best to honor everyone, your chance of a successful celebration rises. Review the book to find more on ways to make it fun for everyone, and don't forget the food. Because we all know that happy and engaged employees have happy tummies!

And speaking of food, remember that **well-being** isn't just a side dish, it's the main course in a solid organization. It's not just the most admired organizations that are looking after their employees' well-being in and out of the office, either. HR directors know that employees become more engaged – and performance and productivity rise – when their well-being (along with that of their families) is looked after.

Other ingredients to create an ideal backdrop for success and celebration in your company: Stay **environmentally conscious**, **socially responsible** and **responsive to the needs of your employees**. A **giving ritual** will make not only others feel better, but yourself as well. What are you passionate about that you can share with others? Take the steps necessary to **bring your passions into the world** in meaningful ways.

Finally, don't be so quick to look through the eyes of 'I'. Instead of focusing inward, **look outside of yourself** and in any situation ask the question, '**How can I create someone else's perfect world**?'

TOWARDS A NEW PARADIGM FOR CELEBRATION

Let's close by looking one last time at our renewed definition of the word 'Celebration'. Hopefully by now you can see that celebration truly is a way of seeing and being. It is indeed **acknowledging all that is good** and recognizing the many passages in our lives which contain seeds of celebration: big and small successes, survival of hard times, lessons learned from failure, the purpose and power of play, personal goals and victories, connecting and collaborating, improving well-being, and honoring our communities.

Remember, when we live in a constant state of celebration, happiness finds a permanent place in our lives. We're around such a short time, why not make the very most of it?

So go on... Tap into the rhythm of your community, and dance alongside your brothers and sisters. There's so much to see, do, and appreciate – especially when we're celebrating every step of the way.

Happy Celebrating!

Scott

PS: We'd like to stay on this journey with you. Stay here and celebrate with us at Facebook – **celebration at work** and at **CelebrationFactor.com.**

Interviewees

Jun Maria Tan Abdullah	Kuala Lumpur	Malaysia	MIMOS
Capt. Mike Abrashoff	Washington D. C.	US	Navy, Retired
AzizRazaq Al Alawi	Kingdom of Bahrain		Electricity & Water Authority
Layla Mohammed Al Sharif	Kingdom of Bahrain		Gulf Air
Celia Alphonsus	Kuala Lumpur	Malaysia	Green Purchasing Asia
George Ang	Kuala Lumpur	Malaysia	Revenue Valley
George Aveling	Kuala Lumpur	Malaysia	TMI
Ellena Balkcom	Orlando, FL	US	Disney
Anirvan Banerjee	Mumbai	India	VOLTAS Limited
Susan Barrett	Englewood, CO	US	National Exchange Carriers
Assn.			
Vikram Bector	Mumbai	India	TATA MOTORS
Scott Bemis	Denver, CO	US	Denver Business Journal
Brenda Bence	Singapore	Singapore	Brenda Bence & Associates
Leonora Billings-Harris, CSP	Greensboro, NC	US	Lenoraspeaks.com
JoAnna Brandi	West Palm Beach, FL	US	Returnonhappiness.com
Sheryl Chamberlain	San Francisco, SF	US	EMC Senior Director
Martha Collard	Hong Kong	China	Lane Crawford
Donald Cooper	Toronto	Canada	DonaldCooper.com
Dorsey Delavigne	Raleigh Durham, NC	US	NetApp
John DiDominic	Bangkok	Thailand	The APM Group
Gary Dragul	Englewood, CO	US	GDA Real Estate
Chester Elton	Summit, NJ	US	The Orange Revolution
JD Franke	Austin,TX	US	The Scooter Store
Brad Friedman	Denver, CO	US	The Friedman Group
Frank Furness	Oxhey, Watford	UK	FrankFurness.com
Gautam Ganglani	Dubai	UAE	Right Selection
Sandip Ghose	Mumbai	India	Reserve Bank of India
Barbara Glanz, CSP, CPAE	Sarasota, FL	US	BarbaraGlanz.com
Tan Chong Guan	Kuala Lumpur	Malaysia	Forever Living Products
Bob Hagey	Orlando, FL	US	Seminole County Govt.
Parveen Hatim	Karachi	Pakistan	Pakistan State Oil Company
Andrew Heard	Bangkok	Thailand	Towers Watson
Charly Heavenrich	Boulder, CO	US	Charlyheavenrich.com
Constant Hine	Denver, CO	US	Horizons in Learning
Barry & Arlene Hirschfeld	Denver, CO	US	AB Hirschfeld & Sons

Odette Huang & Patrick ??	Singapore	Singapore	Royal Plaza on Scotts Hotel
Adrienne Isakovic Ph.D	Abu Dhabi	UAE	Khalifa University
Shanty Jeyabalan	Kuala Lumpur	Malaysia	Dominos Pizza
Kathy Justice	Huntington, Utah	US	Carbon Emery Insurance
Thierry Kennel	Denver, CO	US	Four Seasons Hotels &
Resorts			
MK Key	Nashville, TN	US	mkkey.com
Mel Kleiman	Houston, TX	US	Humetrics Holding, Inc.
Raj Kumar Paramanathan	Kuala Lumpur	Malaysia	CnetG Asia
Freek Kusters	Amsterdam	Netherlands	Etos Netherlands
Erik Laar	Ratum	Netherlands	Yamazaki Mazak Optonics
Callum Laing	Singapore	Singapore	Fitness Buffet
Erik Lehman	Ithaca, NY	US	Dream Catalyst
Theresa Letman	Littleton, CO	US	Verus Global
Helen Lim	Singapore	Singapore	Silverspring
Mary Loverde, CSP, CPAE	Highlands Ranch, CO	US	MaryLoverde.com
Joris Luijke	Sydney	Australia	Atlassian
Phil Mason	Denver, CO	US	Nestle, USA
Kim Mattel	Denver, CO	US	Believe In Yourself Spa
Lloyd Maddock	Karachi	Pakistan	HSBC
Ramola Mahajani	Mumbai	India	TAJ Hotels
Adil Malia	Mumbai	India	ESSAR
Abdulla Yousif Matter	Kingdom of Bahrain		Origin Group
Ian James McDonald	Lahore	Pakistan	Nestle
Dr Abdulhai Megdad	Riyadh	Saudi Arabia	MegaBizs
Jayesh Menon	Kuala Lumpur	Malaysia	Flextronics
Tina Merten	Toledo, WA	US	The Toledo Telephone Co.
SV Nathan	Hyderabad	India	Deloitte
Bob Nelson	San Diego, CA	US	Nelson Motivation, Inc.
Mailie Thomas Ngake	Pretoria	South Africa	PHSDSBC
Ricky Nowak	Melbourne	Australia	RickyNowak.com
Bart Olde Hampsink	Utrecht	Netherlands	Atos Origin
R Palan	Kuala Lumpur	Malaysia	SMR HR Group
Marcel Pitton	Denver, CO	US	Brown Palace
Anneloes Post	Enschede	Netherlands	University of Twente
Lynn Price	Highlands Ranch, CO	US	Camp To Belong
Denise Pushnik	Denver, CO	US	Verus Global
Abeer Qumsieh	Amman	Jordan	Better Business
LaRae Quy	San Francisco, CA	US	Your Best Adventure

Chintamani Rao	New Delhi	India	RK Swamy Media Group
Tom Rath	Washington D.C.	US	Gallup
Alexandra Richardson	Hong Kong	China	PEPSICO
Lynda Reinhart	Gainesville, FL	US	University of Florida
Rick Rios	Anchorage, AK	US	Consultant
Craig Ross	Denver, CO	US	Verus Global
Uwe Rotermund	Dortmund	Germany	Noventum Consulting
Mark Sanborn, CSP, CPAE	Highlands Ranch, CO	US	Mark Sanborn.com
Rodrigo Santos		Brazil	Sicredi
Jolene Selby	Great Falls, Montana	US	Student Assistance
Foundation			
Amar Sinhji	Mumbai	India	TATA Capital
Christa Sorenson	Chicago, IL	US	Equity Residential
Tommy Spaulding	Denver, CO	US	TommySpaulding.com
Kristi Stepp	Singapore	Singapore	Kelly Services
Shayna Stillman	Alexandria, VA	US	Washington Speakers
Bureau			
Linda Swindling, JD, CSP	Dallas, TX	US	lindaswindling.com
Selvi Supuriamaniam	Penang	Malaysia	
David Thomas	Hong Kong	China	Standard Chartered Bank
Fons Trompenaars	Amsterdam	Netherlands	THT Consulting
Zsuzsanna Tungli	Singapore	Singapore	Developing Global Leaders
Bernadette Vadurro	Santa Fe, NM	US	Speakerlive.com
Hans van der Meer	Amsterdam	Netherlands	Microsoft
Steven Vannoy	Denver, CO	US	Versus Global
Ellen Weber	Pittsford, NY	US	MITAWInternational Brain
Based Center			
Mike Wittenstein	Marietta, GA	US	Mikewittenstein.com
Kristie Wolter	Helena, MT	US	Montana Dept of Labor
Che Yaneza	Singapore	Singapore	Mediacorp
Craig Zablocki	Denver, CO	US	Craigzablocki.com
Marcel Pitton	Denver, CO	US	Brown Palace Hotel

Scott Friedman & Associates
16351 W. Ellsworth Ave.
Golden, CO 80401
Phone: 303-284-0811

website: www.ScottFriedman.net
e-mail: Scott@ScottFriedman.net